THE
MYSTERIES
OF THE
INQUISITION.

BY M. V. DE FÉRÉAL.

GEO. PEIRCE,
310, STRAND.

THE
MYSTERIES OF THE INQUISITION.

CHAPTER I.

EL BARRIO DE TRIANA.

BOUT the middle of the sixteenth century, during the reign of Charles the Fifth, the population of Seville, the gay and happy capital of Andalusia, had gradually become silent, dull and melancholy. It was in vain that the city of the Moors, spread out beneath the rays of a glorious sun its vast terraces, covered with shrubs and flowers, its elegant balconies, where green and flowering plants, red pomegranates, and Virginia jasmines, with their large golden corollæ, intermingled like the network of lace.

No longer were heard in the evening, beneath the balconies, the voices of amorous swains, mingled with the shrill notes of the mandolin; and if, during the delicious hours of the night, timid damsels ventured to show themselves on the terraces, and breathe the fresh and perfumed air that rose from the banks of the Guadalquivir, they moved along as silently and solemnly as ghosts, while suppressed sighs alone arose from their noiseless lips, instead of the healthy and merry laugh—that harmonious melody of language from the mouth of women, which causes the Spanish tongue to resemble music.

In every place terror had long since raised his sinister standard; no more family gossipings, no more meetings under the parental roof—distrust and fear paralysed the gentlest sentiments of the heart. The father was suspicious of his son, brother of brother, friend of friend; for at this epoch every one trembled lest he should discover in the being he loved the most, a spy or an informer. No one's life or fortune was safe, men lived on from day to day not daring to form any attachment, and concealing at the bottom of the heart every generous and tender aspiration; finding even no consolation in the hopes of religion, that greatest comforter under every affliction, for they no longer dared to invoke Heaven with a free conscience, uncertain whether their aspirations should be in strictly legal form, and approved of by that supreme tribunal, the INQUISITION! At that time its pitiless tyranny was at its height, and at its head was placed the Cardinal Alphonso Maurique, Archbishop of Seville.

Let us now turn to the 15th of February, 1534.

It was about seven o'clock in the evening, the streets of Seville, formerly so noisy and full of animation, were dark and silent, although it was at the time of the Carnival. At intervals, only, mean-looking monks passed a few straggling gitanos (gipsies), familiars of the Inquisition accosted each other as they crossed with their accustomed sign, and the inhabitants of the Barrio de Triana pressed on towards the avenues leading to the bridge of boats thrown over the Guadalquivir, which united the town to that immense suburb, that filthy sty, where even at the present day the refuse of the population of Seville still pullulate.

Among those who at that hour crossed the bridge of Triana, might have been noticed a man of lofty stature, clothed in the dress of a preaching monk. His ample and serious-looking forehead was rather grave than austere, his large black eyes were full of gentleness, a'though enthusiasm and deep thought caused them to sparkle like fire, and on his silent lips the impress of eloquence and poetry were visible. This man walked slowly, as if wrapped in deep thought; and in the deep abstraction from all terrestrial things in which he was plunged, he noticed not the passers-by who ran against him, nor those against whom he ran in the demi-obscurity of the night. When he had reached the other side of the bridge he stopped for an instant, as if uncertain whether, of the two streets that diverged at this point, he should take that leading to the right or that branching off to the left; but as this indecision was mixed up with his wandering thoughts on some other subject, he remained pensive and motionless on the same spot. He seemed more like a man waiting at a rendezvous, than a philosopher who reflected.

At this instant a well dressed man issued from the right-hand street, which was called la Calle de los Gitanos, or Gipsy-street; and after stopping for a few seconds at the corner of the street, and looking around as if in search of some one, he perceived the monk and walked slowly up to him. When within a few paces of the preacher he again stopped, but still the monk did not notice him. The layman approached to within a pace and whispered—

"*Hita*" (silence), a word by which the familiars of the Inquisition rocognised each other.

At the sound of this voice, the Franciscan suddenly raised his head, looked for an instant at the man who addressed him, and gravely answered "*Corazza*."

"Heaven has directed me to you," added the stranger.

"Heaven is omnipotent," replied the monk.

"Your reverence can follow me," continued the layman.

The monk obeyed, and walked by the side of his guide with as calm and natural an air as if their meeting had been expected; allowing himself to be led like a docile child, and scrupulously observing the imperative silence imposed by the terror inspired by the Inquisition. The stranger and the monk proceeded together along the Calle de los Gitanos, a long black and winding street, in which no light was seen excepting that which proceeded from the numerous taverns that abounded in the whole length of this hideous place, from whence shrill and confused sounds issued, a medley of discordant and drunken voices. The lower orders of Seville, the vile part of the population, rogues and others, were enjoying their revels, and getting drunk with *manzanilla* and *pajarète*, of which they drank deeply out of *chiquitas*, tall slender glasses of a square form, still used in the Andalusian cabarets.

When they reached the end of the street, the layman stopped before a tavern better lighted than the others, and, pointing out the door to his companion, made a sign to him to enter. The monk, without hesitation, crossed the threshold of the horrible den, for it was no rare thing in those days to see men of his order in a tavern, and besides it is a well-known fact that in every age they have mixed themselves up, in Spain, with all that is disgraceful and wicked, and thence arose the contempt and hatred with which they have since that time been pursued.

The preacher then entered the tavern. It was a low room, long and dark, with black smoky walls, marked in various parts with long furrows of a lighter colour, which, cutting up the dark ground, formed a kind of hieroglyphical mosaic. Clumsy and broken-legged benches were placed around the room, before long, black, and filthy tables, which by the constant friction of the elbows of the customers looked as if they were varnished.

On the walls, about half-way from the ceiling, a number of rude pictures, representing the numerous Madonnas worshipped in Spain, had been pasted, together with some of the horrible representations of an *auto-de-fé*. Above each of these pictures two candles, about the thickness of a quill, or a lamp of smoky and stinking oil, were placed. These lights, which were constantly burning, were at night the only source of illumination the room possessed. To the rafters of the ceiling numerous iron hooks with many branches, called *garabatos*, were fixed, from whence hams, bacon, and fresh meat was hanging, as well as men's hats, and even cloaks.

The sight of these hideous-looking men, monks, fortune-tellers, gitanos, and familiars of the Inquisition—for the tavern contained all these varieties—the sight, I say, of these men seated round the long table, in the flickering light of the candles, beneath their strange wardrobe, would make you imagine it was an assembly of demons seated under gibbets in a catacomb. The gray, moist, earthen floor returned no sound beneath the sandals of the monk, and the naked feet of the gitanos; and the sound of their voices resembled a dismal psalmody: the filthy place filled a spectator with disgust and dread. Such at that time were the taverns of the barrio or suburb of Triana.

The preacher seated himself at the extremity of the room, at the end of an unoccupied table; he then invited his companion to place himself near him.

"Directly," said the stranger; "but I must first speak to La Chapa," and he pointed to a young girl who was standing a few paces from them at the door of a recess, which answered the purpose of a kitchen.

La Chapa, the sister of the host, was a young Andalusian brunette, half a gipsy, with delicately rounded limbs, scarcely covered below the calf by a short red petticoat; her long black hair in waving curls, divided into two portions, fell on each side of her head, and reached below her slender waist, and a large mona of orange-coloured riband was fastened above the nape of the neck by means of long and slender pins with polished steel heads, whose numerous facettes shone like so many stars.

The stranger approached her familiarly, and said in a short quick voice and in an under tone—

"Frasco? Has he arrived, Chapa?"

"Not yet" replied the Andalusian girl; "but he cannot be long. I have sent my brother Coco to tell him that Senora Dolores will leave home at midnight; Frasco will soon join you here, as well as this holy man, who is honoured with the confidence of Heaven." And at the same time La Chapa cast a curious glance at the handsome and imposing features of the monk.

"That is the man," said the stranger, the intimate confidant of the very illustrious and reverend father Pedro Arbués; "I met him at the foot of the Triana bridge, as his eminence informed me I should, and we are only waiting for Frasco to complete our business; that is, supposing the Senora Dolores keeps her word."

"She will come out, senor," replied La Chapa; "I myself took her a letter from her intended, which his eminence caused Peter Saavedra (a noted intriguer and forger) to write by way of pastime."

"And the young girl consented at once to the interview?" asked the stranger, whom, to tell our tale more easily, we shall call Enriquez.

"At first she refused," said La Chapa; "but the letter was so pressing! The life of her lover was at stake, and the young maiden promised all I required; she will be at the place of appointment to-night.

You must be certain I know her determination, and I did all in my power to cause her to make up her mind."

"Heaven be praised!" said Enriquez, with a slight feeling of compunction; "you are a real witch, Chapa; and, by my soul, his eminence could not have chosen a better instrument than you to execute his holy and immutable will. You understand, Chapa, that our holy inquisitor has no other end in view than that of rescuing the soul of the maiden from the demon, by preventing her marrying Don Estevan de Vargas, who is, they say, the son of a marrano, and the grandson of a Moor."

"Oh! that is true," said La Chapa, making the sign of the cross. "My lord is a saint, and always acts for the good of Heaven. But do not call me a witch," she added, with a terrified look; "such a word ought not to come out of the mouth of a familiar of the holy office; for in payment for my zeal in the service of the Holy Inquisition, that word might cause me to figure in the first grand auto-de-fé that will take place in honour of the victories of the King, Don Carlos, our well-beloved lord and master."

"Nonsense! be satisfied, Chapa; you are too good a Catholic, and too faithful a servant of the Holy Inquisition, to be suspected. But we shall not be long without an auto-de-fé, and it will not be the first since our beloved lord and king, Don Carlos, mounted the throne; and I promise you you shall have the best seat in the grand balcony in the Plaza Major, to see those heretic dogs roasted."

"Shall I though?" cried the young Andalusian girl, clapping her hands joyfully. "Oh! Senor Enriquez, they say there will be more than fifteen heretics burned, and a great number will be pardoned by his eminence, if they will abjure their faith, and die good Christians: these are to be strangled before they are burned. Oh! how delightful it will be, Senor Enriquez! and you will let me see all, won't you?"

"I swear I will; and it will be magnificent," continued the familiar, delighted to see the gitana so animated, in her zeal for the holy office. But if he had carefully noticed the features of the Andalusian girl, he would have seen that her ruby lips grew imperceptibly pale, and that her eye, so bright and shining, became filled with a vague look of terror, and he might almost have heard her heart beat hurriedly and irregularly beneath her black velvet corset. The sister of Coco could not, when she looked back to her ancestors, discover that the pure Catholic blood of her family was of sufficiently ancient date to make her comfortable with respect to the Inquisition, whose humble servant she was, through fear; and not thoroughly satisfied by the mild and hypocritical look of the soldier of the church, she spoke in an exalted tone, which she endeavoured to render joyful.

"Oh! how delightful it will be! how delightful!"

At this instant she perceived that the large black eyes of the preacher were fixed upon her. The monk had not lost a single word of her conversation, nor the slightest change in the expression of her countenance.

"Bring us some wine, my girl," said the familiar.

And poor Chapa, too happy to avoid the piercing glance of the monk, and the conversation, during which she trembled every instant for fear she should betray her terror—Chapa, light and active, fetched a jug of wine, which she placed before his reverence.

While Enriquez was bringing forward a wooden stool, that he might take his seat in front of the Franciscan, another man entered the tavern. The new comer approached the familiar, and directed his look to the monk.

" Is this our holy commissioner ?" he asked, in honeyed accents.

" Himself, Senor Frasco," replied Enriquez.

The monk rose, and crossed his hands over his breast ; the new comer did the same. The monk crossed his hands in the opposite direction, then he bent towards Frasco, as if in salutation ; Frasco, on his side, did the same, so that their foreheads gently touched each other. This was the peculiar mode of salutation of the familiars of the holy office. But Frasco did not confine himself to these signs of recognition ; he uncovered his breast, and underneath his dress he exhibited a plate of silver, on which was seen the image of an inverted crucifix. The Franciscan made no corresponding sign.

Frasco cast a look of dark suspicion on Enriquez ; Enriquez shrugged his shoulders, with a careless and satisfied look.

" He is not one of us," murmured Frasco, in an under tone.

Enriquez gave a dubious look.

" He is not one of us, I tell you," repeated Frasco, " and we are betrayed ! Betrayed ! do you understand ?" and he grasped the hand of Enriquez forcibly, while his sinister countenance had an expression of ferocious rage.

All this was said in a low tone, but not so low as to prevent the frequenters of the tavern perceiving a movement that announced a quarrel. All eyes were directed on the monk, who remained calm and unmoved, and seemed more like a spectator than an actor in this strange scene.

A few among the guests, when they looked at the Franciscan, whose imposing features inspired respect—a few among them ventured to murmur, and threats against Enriquez and Frasco were uttered by the bandits.

Although certain of vengeance in case of insult, the familiars of the Inquisition had no inclination for a quarrel with the inhabitants of the Barrio de Triana. They knew them well enough to be aware that in defence of a monk they would allow themselves to be cut to pieces to the last man ; but there was that which had a greater power over the people than even monks or priests—*the Inquisition !*

With infernal cunning Frasco then turned towards the drinkers, whose looks and gestures showed their hostile intentions. " Brothers," he cried, " are you such bad Catholics as to defend an enemy of the Inquisition ?"

At this terrible word " Inquisition," you might have seen every head droop, and a livid paleness remove all animation from their features ; you would have said a thunderbolt had fallen in the midst of these rude and turbulent men. No one dared to utter a single word.

Then the preacher, without noticing Frasco's anger, or the stupefaction of the bandits of the tavern, gravely arose, and moved towards the door, in the midst of a mournful silence.

"What!" exclaimed Frasco, "will you let him escape in this manner? Will no one go and inform the officers of the Inquisition?"

"I! I!" cried Chapa, terrified, and at the same time she sprang towards the door, wishing by her zeal to escape the danger in which she always felt herself; but as she was about to lift the latch, the Franciscan cast a long and penetrating look upon her, and La Chapa, fascinated, clasped her hands, and fell on her knees before the holy man. By a simul-

taneous impulse the bandits stretched out their hands towards him, as if to implore his protection against the secret power they dared not brave. Then the monk, turning with a majestic air towards the mute and cowed assembly, blessed them with a heavenly look, and rushing into the street, disappeared before even Frasco himself had thought of detaining him.

"We are deceived, and by your imprudence," said Frasco, addressing Enriquez, who, like the rest, was in a state of profound stupefaction.

"He knows nothing," replied Enriquez.

"Well, then, to work," cried Frasco, re-assured; "we have no need of a third person in this business."

And the two soldiers of the church left the tavern together.

II.

CHAPTER II.

THE PALACE OF THE GARDUNA.

T the extremity of the Barrio de la Triana there stood an ancient building in the Moorish style, the ruins of which served as a place of refuge for the birds of night. Mendicants without an asylum, and thoughtless gitanos often slept amongst the broken masonry during those sultry nights which, in Andalusia, render all shelter unnecessary; and on wintry days, old women, crouching in the sun, sought shelter behind its ruins against the piercing northern winds.

From the magnitude of the dismantled walls, and certain architectural ornaments still in perfect preservation, it was easily seen that a vast and sumptuous mansion must have formerly existed on the spot; for in the midst of the fragments a long, elegant, and light colonnade supported a dome covered with arabesque ornaments, in a state of high preservation; a wall, almost uninjured, although its construction was apparently slight, enclosed this colonnade, which must once have adorned a splendid chamber, and a door of remarkable strength protected the entrance. In various parts among the rubbish, a few wild shrubs were growing; grasses with pale rose-coloured blossoms, bunches of sweet-scented yellow wallflowers, and clumps of eglantine and wild laurels, whose thick bushes cast their shadowy, yet lively verdure, over the nakedness of the ruins. This singular spot served as a place of meeting for the assemblies of the members of the brotherhood of the Garduna; it was, in fact, the palace of the master of the order.

All those who have read the novels of Cervantes must recollect the delightfully grotesque character of the rogue Monipodia, the chief of the thieves of Seville. At the time of which we are speaking, that is to say more than fifty years before Cervantes, a band of robbers, protected by some of the authorities of the police, existed in Spain. This strange institution, the origin of which is dated at the beginning of the fifteenth century, had for its chief, at Seville, a man of strange aspect; at the same time serious and sarcastic, his language was hideously picturesque, the traditional type in other respects, at least as far as character extends, of what was still found in Spain in 1821.

On the same evening in 1534, when the matters we have related in the previous chapter occurred, a scene not less curious, and much more original, took place in the palace of the master of the Garduna. It was about ten o'clock, the heavy and massive door of the palace of the Garduna, turning on its hinges, made way for the entrance of some thirty individuals, of both sexes, and all ages. They entered silently, and in perfect order, scrupulously observing the rights of rank of their hierarchy.

In the centre of the hall, tolerably well lighted by torches fixed in sockets attached to the pillars, stood the master of the order. He was a man of lofty stature, strong and bony; his olive-coloured countenance, marked with numerous scars, had a singular mixture of cunning, audacity, and self-possession, and at times when he deigned to smile, of sarcasm and irony. His masculine and deep-toned voice possessed an energetic power, and when he commanded, the force of his will gave his look and gesture a domineering air. He wore a coarse cloth shirt, and a brown jacket or cloak thrown over his shoulder like a mantle, and zaraguelles, a kind of cloth trousers, that reached as low as the knee. His naked and sinewy legs were covered with hair, and his broad flat and rugged feet, indicating his base extraction and incalculable physical strength, were shod with alpargatas, a kind of sandals fastened round the ankles by a number of strings. This man was called Mandamiento.

The company who had entered the room formed themselves in a circle round the master of Garduna el Florio (theft and assassination).

Near to him, and next in desert, stood, one on the right and the other on the left, two guapos in the prime of life. The first was called Manofina (quick hand), on account of his unequalled skill in dealing a blow with a dagger in passing, so that his victim knew not from whence the blow came, and for his prodigious skill as a swordsman and good shot with the pistol. The other was called Cuerpo de Hierro (frame of iron): he had endured the "question" three times, without acknowledging his crimes, without accusing any one, and without his body appearing to suffer. Lastly, there were two old men called fuelles (whisperers), a name the society gave to such of its members as happily possessing a pleasing exterior, acted as spies and pilots wherever a theft was to be committed. Then there were old women, useful personages called coberteras (fences) in various dresses; and, finally, many young women, called serenas (sirens), who were the bayaderes of the head men of the order. In addition to this, it was their duty to render, by means of their charms, justices, prosecutors, and even lawyers favourable, for on these men the life of the brothers of the Garduna often depended. Frequently also their seductive manners were not powerless in the ease of some voluptuous canon, or loose-minded prior, whose influence in those days was unbounded, both in temporal and spiritual matters. Outside this circle, and at a short distance from it, a young man modestly stood, the principal cause of this meeting, he was called Garabato (a kind of Robert Macaire, a universal rogue).

Senor Mandamiento cast a commanding glance over the audience, devoutly crossed himself, and mumbled a prayer, at the same time turning towards a rude image of the Virgin fixed against the wall. All those present imitated him. Then Mandamiento spoke as follows :—

"Noble and valiant chevaliers of the poniard, faithful fuelles, useful coberteras, seductive serenas, light-limbed chivatos (novices), and the rest of this honourable fraternity, may Heaven grant us its divine protection, and deliver us from all alguazils, executioners, and all those pains and penalties that are often mortal to you, and always dangerous to our brethren. I have called you together to-day to consult you on a circumstance in which our rights are involved, and which may compromise our society. You are all aware, my children, that ever since, by the favour of Heaven, you have laboured under my direction, we have never had occasion to deplore more than a dozen hangings, about forty rides on the back of an ass (a substitute for the pillory), and a few engagements in the royal marine (the galleys). Seville furnished every year six times that number of punishments before you elected me chief of your fraternity. Scarcely seventy-five gauchos (robbers), half of whom are new hands, have fallen into the lion's mouth, and out of some thirty of our brethren now within its power, I can affirm that scarcely three will be hung, five or six sent to the galleys, and a dozen placed in the pillory; there may be about three or four flogged, and about as many of our sisters passed through the honey-pot; but we have not been able to prevent it. But when we shall have money enough to have more masses said, and to pay the alguazils better, our affairs will proceed in a different manner. Such is the flourishing state of the Garduna, at present, my children."

[The punishment of passing through the honey-pot was as follows:— The culprit stripped to the waist, was placed on the back of an ass, with a conical cap on her head, she had her body smeared with honey, and, with a chain round her neck, she was led through the streets by the executioner with a file of soldiers on each side; the cause of her punishment was then frequently declared, and each time this was done, a handful of feathers was thrown over her, until at length she became completely covered with them.]

"If I recall my slight services to you," continued Mandamiento, with feigned modesty, "it is not to make a parade of the feeble talent bestowed upon me by Heaven, whose humble instrument I am; but to make you understand how important the closest union is to us, that the most perfect agreement should exist among us, to enable us to exercise our useful profession with the greatest possible success, and deserve the esteem of the lords and ladies who do us the honour of employing us. I will now speak of the cause of this meeting."

At the same time the master looked round him with a scrutinizing eye, and perceiving Garabato, who was leaning in a humble manner against a column, he made a sign to him to approach. Garabato hastened to obey him. The living circle that intervened between him and the master opened to allow him to pass. The young man advanced, and, after taking a few steps, he found himself close to Senor Mandamiento. The master of the Garduna took the young man by the hand, and showing him to the assembly, continued—

"Brothers, the lords of Manofina and Cuerpo de Hierro surprised this young man under the peristyle of the cathedral, stealing the pocket handkerchief of a gentleman, and then a well-filled purse from the pocket of the sacristan of a convent of nuns.   To say the truth, this was all very cleverly done, but it is not the less true, that as he does not belong to our fraternity, he has violated the statutes of our order by robbing without authority, and more than that, by attacking the goods of the church.   The lords Manofina and Cuerpo de Hierro, in consideration of the good disposition and the precocious talent of the young man—a talent, they say, that will do honour to the Garduna, Heaven and our good lessons assisting him—Manofina and Cuerpo de Hierro have thought it better to bring him to us, than to carry him before the beaks, who would perhaps have stifled his promising talent.   But for all this, the young man has infringed our statutes, and deserves to be peached. What is your opinion, gentlemen ?" said Mandamiento, looking round the assembly.

"The master is right," murmured the bandits; "the young fellow deserves to be peached."

Manofina and Cuerpo de Hierro gave a low and discontented growl.

"Cursed canaille," grumbled Manofina; "it is the same as at Rosario, they always answer 'Amen!'"

"Such an excellent cut-purse!" added Cuerpo de Hierro.

"Peach him! peach him!" repeated several of the fences at the same time, showing, like laughing hyænas, two or three long and jagged teeth, which hung over their lower lip, like the tusks of a wild boar.

Mandamiento remained unmoved, but nothing that passed around him had escaped his notice; he allowed the disturbance to subside of its own accord, and then again addressing the assembly—

"What is your opinion, gentlemen ?" he said, in a voice having more the tone of command than that of deference.

Everybody was silent, and their stupid looks had that expression of passive and instinctive obedience which vulgar minds always yield to men of capacity.   The two guapos alone, cast a sidelong glance at their leader, full of discontent and hatred.   The master appeared not to perceive it, and turning once more to the assembly—

"Gentlemen," he said, "my advice is, that on account of the precocious talents of this young man, and also in consideration of our much-honoured brothers, Manofina and Cuerpo de Hierro, who patronise him, that we should receive this young man among us as a brother postulant, dispensing with his year of noviciate; and that the better to encourage him we should grant him all the privileges to which such of our apprentices are entitled, who have distinguished themselves during their year of trial, on condition that he pays all the dues the other brothers pay to the fraternity, and makes his offering to the church.   In a word, I take him under my protection.   And now," added the grand master, in a loud voice, "if any of you have any observations to make, let them speak."

They were all silent, but some of the serenas looked kindly on the young Garabato, for he was a very good-looking lad.

"Stupid brutes," murmured the guapos.

"It is well, gentlemen," continued Mandamiento; "your wishes are in accordance with mine, and I thank you."

Then advancing to Garabato, he again took him by the hand, and presented him to those present, individually, and each man gave him the fraternal embrace ; the grand master did him the same honour, and he then gave him the password, and taught him the different signs and grips of their order; finally, he handed him a parchment, on which the duties and privileges of the brothers of the Garduna were written.

The ceremony over, Garabato mixed himself with his new companions in murder and theft.

Then the master drawing from his pocket a dirty piece of paper, covered with writing, like hieroglyphics—

"Brothers," he said, "this is the order of the day. Three baptisms (poniard wounds), to be applied as gently as possible ; one on a handsome young fellow, with black moustaches, who passes every evening, at seven o'clock, over the bridge of Triana. He is a tall, good-looking hidalgo, and wears a scarlet cloak. Fifty réals will be paid for this baptism, and five hundred maravedis in addition, if it can be applied on the face, so as to mark my man well. The party who pays for it is a lady, still handsome, and tolerably young ; so, Senor Garabato, I rely on your gallantry for the fair sex, for you are entrusted with this business. Thus you will have to receive thirty-seven réals and a half, without calculating the five hundred maravedis the lady will give you, if you can manage to mark his face with an indelible scratch—an easy affair, for you will only have to rub the wound you make with a little soot mixed with vinegar ;" and Mandamiento gave Garabato a phial filled with a blackish kind of liquor. "The second baptism," continued the master, "will only be forty réals : it is to be administered to his Paternity, the prior of the convent of La Merci ; he has carried a female penitent from his Beatitude, the father provincial. His Beatitude will pay for it ; he will give a bonus of four doubloons, if we succeed in destroying the eye of the prior, for the penitent in question loves nothing in the world so much as fine eyes. I think we can be certain of the four doubloons. I must give this baptism to Senor Manofina and his darling Culervina, who, by her cunning, will be able to bring the prior of La Merci to a fitting place for the business. That will be thirty réals," he added, "and don't forget the Holy Virgin ; the four doubloons will belong to the serena."

"Yes, yes ; I'll undertake the task," cried the serena, the master called by the name of Culervina. "I'll undertake it, Senor Mandamiento!"

"Silence, my wild rose," said the master, twisting his moustache, "we know your skill and devotedness. A real jewel you have there, my son," he continued, turning to the guapo ; "take care of her, and don't beat her too much."

"Yes, a pretty jewel, to be kept for the pleasure of others," murmured the bandit, with a brutal expression of jealousy.

"Come, come, Senor Manofina, be more devoted to our common cause."

The Garduna was silent, but he looked at the serena with suspicion and anger. Culervina came close to him, and passing her arm within his, she looked tenderly in his face with her large and brilliant eyes.

"Come, my dear Manofina, don't be angry now ; you know I love none but you."

The features of the guapo assumed a milder expression, and he yielded to the power of that passion which is omnipotent over natures of his temperament.

"You love me, then," he said, in a whisper, "do you, truly? But, this prior?"

"Well, this prior, I'll bring him to you, that's all. I don't mind breaking a promise to him; you know I am yours only."

The guapo looked at her with a mingled expression of happy confidence and painful suspicion; and strangely enough, the serena told the truth. By a rare exception, this woman had sworn to perform the most libertine acts, employed her marvellous beauty to seduce victims into the snares of the Garduna, but neither her heart nor her person were accomplices in her forced duties; she had always, and in every point, remained faithful to the ill-tempered guapo she had chosen for her lover.

Mandamiento continued—

"The third baptism receives six doubloons; a canon pays for it, you may know that by the price: this baptism is to be administered to a brother canon before six in the evening, that he may not be able to visit the members of the chapter, to solicit their votes for the election of dean, thus giving his rival a better chance. If, after a few days, this baptism should be changed into a burial, the canon will give double the sum, but it must be always understood, it must be done skilfully, so as not to let the man croak at once; such is the desire of the applicant, who pays well that he may be well served. Besides this, if the canon should be elected dean, the Garduna may calculate on his protection; his *seigneurie* has made me a formal promise. This baptism will be your business Senor Cuerpo de Hierro; make use of a slender poignard, or better still, one with a triangular blade, or a bodkin, unless you have a good saddler's needle—that would be the best instrument to make a wound that would not be fatal for a few days, and one that would not bleed. There is your money, now be off, and be particular."

"Six *baths* (drownings) are to be administered, and these will be easy jobs for six of the common men. In addition to this, there are three *voyages*, (highway robberies) one on the road to Jaen, to-morrow, at nine o'clock; a *galera* (the post) will pass at that time, the bearer of eighty thousand réals, for the nuncio of his Holiness, the produce of the sale of indulgences in the kingdom of Seville; another, on the road to San-Lucar, at midnight; also, to intercept a galera, the bearer of one hundred and twenty-five thousand réals, for a Moorish banker, at Seville. It is our duty to take this money out of the hands of the enemies of the church, who can only employ it to the detriment of our holy religion. The third voyage is to take place on the road to Grenada, where it branches off to Xeres; three gentlemen will pass that way with well-lined purses, and a new wardrobe, and many of our brethren are very badly togged. These three expeditions were entrusted to three safe men of the brotherhood, passed masters. Finally," said Mandamiento, and this is a serious affair, an *obscurcissement* (assassination) on the person of Don Estevan de Vargas, who leaves the house of his Exellency the Governor of Seville every night, at twelve o'clock. They say he is to be married to his daughter, a handsome girl, seventeen years of age,

and this obscurcissement will be the cause of many tears, but that is no
business of ours; this operation is to be paid for by fifty doubloons in
advance, and the same amount if we are successful, together with the
protection of the very reverend the Inquisitor of Seville, who is no doubt
interested in the affair, since he has offered us his protection, a species
of coin of which he is not very prodigal."

"And what guarantee have we for his fair promises?" said Manofina,
who had been strangely affected at the fate of the two lovers, by the
glances and caresses of his serena.

At this instant, a chivato, who was on the watch at a short distance
from the ruins, ran in with a terrified look—

"Master! Master!" he exclaimed, "here is a *corchette* (police-officer)
coming to the house."

The Gardunas in alarm, placed their hands on their daggers, but the
master remained unmoved, and turning to his companions, said—

"To your knees, children," and then looking at the image of the Virgin, he began devoutly to count his beads, his companions giving the
responses in a loud tone.

A few minutes afterwards, the alguazil half opened the door, and thrust
his head into the room. Mandamiento, without discontinuing his prayer,
turned his head slowly towards him, and, in the very middle of his Ave
Maria, exclaimed joyfully—

"It is our trusty brother, Coco."

A general sign of the cross brought the prayers to an abrupt conclusion; every body rose, and the captain, drawing the alguazil into a
corner of the room, said—

"What has brought you here, brother Coco? do you know of any
danger threatening our society?"

"Not exactly," replied the corchette, "you know I keep a good look
out, and that my double duties as alguazil and familiar of the Holy
Office, give me an opportunity of saving you from many a snare."

"Quite true, you are a good friend, and a devoted brother."

"Well, then, master," continued Coco, "it is in your power to do me
a service in return."

"Speak, brother, what is the business?"

"In the first place," continued the alguazil, "you must return one of
my relations, the sacristan of the Carmelites, the purse he was robbed of
this morning."

"You shall have the purse, brother; we are ready to satisfy you on
that subject. What next?"

"The next is a more serious affair," said the corchette, lowering his
voice, "it is nothing less than the obscurcissement, in case of necessity,
of two or three of the familiars of the Holy Inquisition."

"Brother!" cried Mandamiento, with a terrified air, "you abuse your
position. You are asking impossible things."

"Impossible or not, they must be done," said Coco, in a firm voice.

"But are you not aware, brother, that the Holy Inquisitor of Seville
is our best employer?"

"It matters not, you must serve me, or after to-day I am no longer
one of you," said the alguazil, resolutely.

"Well, then, what must be done?" asked the captain, overcome by this menace.

"You must let me have, without delay, two or three tried guapos, and about half-a-dozen chivatos, to lead them where I think fit, that they may quiet whom I wish; and, finally, that they may obey my orders in every thing, as they do yours."

"You ask too much, Coco."

"The apostle requires it," replied the alguazil, drily; "make haste, then; Mandamiento; hasten, for there is no time to lose."

"Since the apostle requires it, we must obey," said the master, sighing, "his will must be obeyed, like that of Heaven, for he restored Manofina to life, and delivered Cuerpo de Hierro from the lion's jaws, and he cures our disorders. Be it as you wish, Coco, take my two best guapos, and let them obey you as they would myself."

At the same time, the master made a sign to Cuerpo de Hierro, and said a few words to him, in a low voice; then calling to Manofina, he desired them to accompany the alguazil.

"I forgot to tell you," he added, addressing Manofina, "that I give to you the task of silencing young Estevan; that operation will restore you to the good graces of the Inquisitor, in case of any check in the business you are about to undertake for Coco. Adieu, senores, keep up your spirits."

Each of the two bravoes chose three active and sturdy chivatos.

III.

"Go!" cried the master, waving his hand, "may the Virgin protect you."

The alguazil placed himself at their head, and favoured by the darkness, the little troop silently left the cave of the Garduna.

CHAPTER III.

DOLORES.

AN incident of a different nature occurred in the house of the governor of Seville, while this horrible and strange scene was taking place in the palace of the Garduna. It was one of those vast and commodious Andalusian buildings, lighted only by glass doors and windows, and opening on a large garden filled with flowers.

In the upper story of the house, the usual winter residence, close to a large room in which the family assembled, was a little chamber, furnished like the cell of a nun— a small bed, white and hard, with plain batiste curtains, carved ebony chairs, a *prie-Dieu* in the same style, surmounted by a large ivory crucifix, and in a recess (a kind of niche formed in the wall), a small statue of the Virgin, in white marble, from the chisel of a celebrated sculptor, before which a lamp of silver gilt, filled with the purest olive oil, was constantly burning. This chamber belonged to the governor's daughter.

The youthful maiden, for she was scarcely seventeen years of age, was far from resembling the rest of the Andalusian women. Possessed of great beauty, at the same time of a simple and noble nature, Dolores had not passed her youthful years in that mystic idleness which so immoderately excites the passions and the imaginations of the Spanish women. Her preceptor was her maternal uncle, a learned and serious man, who, having travelled much in France and Germany, had striven to cultivate her brilliant intellect and strengthen her philosophy. Nor had he cast the seeds of knowledge on a barren soil; Dolores, even in our time, would have been a remarkable woman.

Ardent both in heart and soul, possessed of exquisite judgment, strong reasoning powers, and energetic will, her faith was as pure and enlightened as that of the fathers of the church, and she rejected all the errors and cruelties of fanaticism. Her piety equalled that of Isabella the Catholic, that great queen, who, filled with horror, strove so long against the establishment of the Inquisition and its subsequent proceedings. Still, notwithstanding her knowledge, so far in advance of her age and of the times in which she lived, Dolores, constant to all the external forms of religion, and the daughter of good Catholics, had not hitherto drawn upon herself the notice of the terrible tribunal. The Grand Inquisitor of Seville, Pierre Arbues, seemed, on the contrary, to extend his all-powerful friendship to the house of the governor, as a pledge of peace. Received in the family at all hours, in his double character of priest and chief of the inquisitorial tribunal, Pierre Arbues, at that time of life when the passions are unbridled—he was scarcely forty—could not look upon the pure and holy girl without feeling for her an unholy passion; nor could he see without horrible jealousy the young Estevan de Vargas become the only object of the affection of the daughter of the governor of Seville. He had marked the progress of this passion with painful uneasiness, and a hatred so deep, that with all his cunning as a priest of the Inquisition he could scarcely conceal it.

In vain, beneath the cloak of holy and fatherly friendship, had he endeavoured to excite in the mind of the beautiful girl feelings in accordance with his own; vainly had he essayed the fascination of his look, and of his really handsome features.

Dolores, when in his company, was never able to suppress a feeling of fear, which she endeavoured to persuade herself was respect; the look of the Inquisitor troubled her to such an extent, as to make her grow pale and tremble.

On the day of which we are speaking, Pierre Arbues had passed the evening with the governor.

About ten o'clock, the maiden, uneasy and agitated, had just retired to her chamber, she simply latched her door, according to her common practice, having nothing to fear in her father's house, where she was adored by all; untying her head-gear she let her long tresses descend upon her alabaster shoulders, and kneeling down prayed fervently. Thus for a few minutes she gave vent to the deep despair that oppressed her soul, then drawing a letter from her bosom, she read it with sorrowful eagerness,—

"It is, yes it is his writing. Poor Estevan, I did not then deceive myself, the Inquisition hates him, and he feared to compromise me by coming here. The journey which he told me was so absolutely necessary was but a pretext to absent himself for a few days; and yet he cannot exist without seeing me, and he begs of me to be this evening at the foot of the Giralda (a statue with a vane at the summit), where he will wait for me; he will die if I refuse him. Oh! yes, he will die without me, and I shall also die, deprived of him," she added, wiping away a tear; "our affection cannot be extinguished by absence. Oh, Heaven!" she exclaimed, "in what unhappy days do we live, when the gentlest feelings of our nature must be suppressed! From what cause has this age of iron arisen, in which even the worship of Heaven is restricted; in which the priests are no longer our comforters, but our butchers, and the tree of life, like a tree of death, spreads its funereal branches over the world? Oh! Estevan, to what friendly country can we fly together, where this leprosy has not spread?" And in a fit of wild despair the unhappy girl wrung her hands, sprung towards the ivory crucifix that surmounted her *prie-Dieu*, and pressed it against her breast. All at once, by a sudden re-action, heart-rending sobs agitated her frame, and she covered the image she clasped, with her bitter tears.

At this instant some one gently opened the door of her oratory, and the unhappy Dolores arose in terror, and drew back as far as the window, at the sight of the Grand Inquisitor himself, who, clothed in his large cloak, slowly advanced towards her. Dolores had not even strength enough to scream.

"I interrupt you at your devotion, my child?" said Pierre Arbues, in a gentle voice.

"My lord," she said, in broken accents, "why do you enter my room thus, at night; the chamber of a young female ought to be sacred?"

"The Grand Inquisitor has full power of dispensation," replied the Dominican, "and you commit no sin in receiving me into your room."

"My lord," replied Dolores, scarlet with pride and indignation, "I do not understand this miserable sophistry that limits the immutable laws of conscience at the will of him who employs it, that makes that blameless in one which is criminal in another. Virtue is unchangeable, and her laws ought to be invariable and eternal. You are a man, my lord, and a man ought not to enter a female's apartment at night, unless it be her husband."

"Dolores," said the Inquisitor, in a harsh tone, "know you not that the Scriptures have given us complete power over soul and body?"

"My lord, do not misrepresent their meaning; there is but one mode of understanding them; the same for all—for the priest and for his flock."

"You are imprudent, maiden, in venturing to speak thus in my presence. The holy books are a sacred code, the interpretation of which belongs to us. Evil fall on those who interpret them without resorting to us! Evil be to those who madly rush into error and heresy! If you had spoken thus before any other than the Grand Inquisitor of Seville," continued Pierre Arbues, with a terrible look, "to-morrow's sun would not have found you in your father's house, and the Inquisition——"

"I have done nothing against the Inquisition," said the affianced bride of Estevan, in a voice she strove to render firm, while an irrepressible feeling of terror made her tremble in spite of herself.

Pierre Arbues perceived it, and approached the young girl, who could not retreat further, as her feet touched the wall beneath the window.

"Dolores," he said, "know you not I am your friend?"

"Oh! my lord, leave me, and do not abuse your power by violating my home in this manner. Go, my lord, go; I entreat you on my knees."

Pierre Arbues, wrapt in the contemplation of her marvellous beaut

DOLORES REPULSING THE INQUISITOR.

seemed not to hear her prayer. Dolores was there before him, her long hair dishevelled, dressed in a black robe, which deeply sloped at the neck, according to the fashion of the day, contrasted admirably with the pure and graceful contour of her alabaster shoulders. Her lofty form seemed still more proud and stately, and the brilliancy of her large dark eyes, in which the whole of her life seemed to have taken refuge, gave a new charm to the striking palor of her features.

"Oh! child," cried the priest, "oh! child, how beautiful you are, and how happy is Estevan!"

"My lord," said Dolores, alarmed at the expression of the Dominican's features; "my lord, am I dreaming? Are you no longer the Grand Inquisitor of Seville, the priest of Heaven, the guardian of the virtue of others?"

"No!" exclaimed the monk, carried away by the fierce flame that devoured him; "it is no Grand Inquisitor, no priest—it is Pierre Arbues, who adores you; Pierre Arbues, who is dying of despair and love!"

A harsh inarticulate sound issued from the breast of the maiden, and her form became as cold as a block of marble.

The Inquisitor was on his knees, and the violence of his brutal passion had for the instant made his naturally handsome and regular features horrible; he endeavoured to lay hold of the governor's daughter, who in the extremity of her fear drew herself up so close to the wall, that she seemed to escape from the trembling hands of the Dominican, like a shadow;—now he touched the hem of her garment, and Dolores, incapable of retreating, remained rigid and petrified before the narrow window. But still, as in the attitude in which the unworthy priest had found her, she pressed the ivory crucifix against her breast; and the instant the Inquisitor, emboldened by her terror, threw his arms round her waist, she energetically extended towards him the holy symbol.

"Pierre Arbues," she exclaimed, "pass this boundary if you dare! Priest of Heaven, dare you brave your Master?"

The villanous Dominican lowered his head, and drew back—he was terrified. The fanatical priest dared to violate the laws of God, but dared not to profane an image. He slowly arose, cast a look of intense hatred on the young girl, and left the room without looking back.

Dolores again pressed her protector image to her bosom. The dismal voice of the watch cried half-past eleven; and although completely exhausted, Estevan's affianced bride fastened up her hair with a large tortoiseshell comb, enveloped herself in a long brown cape, descended softly the stone steps leading to the outer door of the house, and took the road to the Giralda.

As she passed the threshold of her house an indistinct shadow was projected from an arcade; it gradually increased in size upon the wall, feebly lighted by a dismal lamp, and distinctly exhibited the profile of a man, enveloped in a cloak. Dolores started, but she continued to walk on without stopping.

"Good," said the Inquisitor, for he it was; "she has gone out: Enriquez will do the rest."

CHAPTER IV.

LA GIRALDA.

THE little troop, under the guidance of Coco, having left the cave of the Garduna, silently followed the provisional chief assigned to them. The guapos went first, on either side of Coco, the chivatos followed in the rear, gliding along the buildings of the dark and tortuous street, and speaking no more than if mankind had been dumb from infancy.

In France we can do nothing without making a great noise; in Spain it is a very different thing indeed. The Spaniard acts without speaking, without any outward demonstration of feeling, his looks explain nothing, you might as well strike a statue, it would merely return a dull sound, and you can never guess at the stormy feelings within that marble breast.

Culervina followed a little behind, alarmed at the secret mission entrusted to Manofina, uneasy with regard to the rude man she loved, and perhaps, also, drawn onward by that womanish instinct, that irresistibly leads the sex wherever there is grief to assuage, or danger to avert.

Coco and his troop went on in this manner as far as the bridge of Triana, then passed through several narrow and obscure streets, and arrived at last at the square of the esplanade, near the cathedral. The spot was extremely dark, and all the lights were out in the neighbouring houses. It is true the twinkling stars shone in the sky, but these radiant orbs, too far removed from us, quietly rolled on in space, not deigning to allow their sparkling light to reach the earth, bestowed no doubt on creatures more happy than those of our melancholy planet.

Having reached the cathedral, Coco caused the two guapos to conceal themselves in a recess between two enormous columns, he then whispered a few words to the young chivatos, who immediately posted themselves at the four angles of the esplanade, where they lay flat on the ground, with their ear close to the earth that the slightest sound might not escape them. Having disposed his party in this manner, Coco directed his steps towards the great door of the cathedral, and in his turn chose a place of concealment beneath its massive masonry.

The serena, fearful of being seen, followed the line of houses that surrounded the esplanade, and walked with so light a step that you might have imagined she was borne upon invisible wings; then gliding between the trees, she stopped at last beneath a large orange tree, near the fountain. At the slight noise made by the serena, a shrill cry like that of a cricket was heard at one of the angles of the square; but everything relapsing again into deep silence, Coco imagined it was a false alarm, and no one moved. At this moment the watch crossed the esplanade, and, stopping near the fountain, cried twelve o'clock in a hoarse monotonous voice. The serena started. Midnight! the hour of crime; the hour in which the miserable woman had been a witness or actor in so many sanguinary scenes—the hour at which the shadows of those she had seen murdered appeared before her eyes. She was terrified. The watch passed on, and she heard nothing but the scarcely distinguishable rustling of the leaves, as they were agitated by the breeze. The serena knelt and prayed. But a light quick step was soon heard on the sand in the direction of the Giralda; one of the chivatos uttered a sharper cry than the former one, and it was instantly repeated by the other three. Coco, Manofina, and Cuerpo de Hierro placed their hands on their poniards. The serena rose, and stretched out her neck to see from which side the danger came, and at that instant Dolores crossed the esplanade. When she arrived at the foot of the Giralda, she looked round her in every direction, and perceiving no one, she called out in a low voice " Estevan! Estevan!" No one answered.

But at the same moment a young woman issued from the tower in a state of alarm, and threw herself at the feet of the governor's daughter.

" Who are you? and what is it you want?" said Dolores.

" Fly! fly hence!" said la Chapa, for she it was; " fly, senora, you are betrayed, I deceived you."

" But where is Estevan?" said the young girl, recognising the voice of her who had brought the forged letter of her lover to her.

" I know nothing about it," answered la Chapa, completely overwhelmed with shame, " I do not know him."

" You do not know him? and yet you told me he would wait for me here this evening?"

" I deceived you," replied the gitano; " they said to me, go! and I was obliged to go. As for me, alas! I am but a miserable instrument, I was obliged to do it through fear of my life—but when I saw you so noble and beautiful, I swore to save you although I should perish; fly then, senora, fly I conjure you—it will soon be too late—they are coming."

But Dolores, completely bewildered, saw not her own danger, she thought only of Estevan pursued by the Inquisition, and the doubt in which she was left caused her inexpressible anguish.

Suddenly a dull rolling sound, accompanied by a slight trampling noise, was heard near the banks of the river. The cricket cry of the chivatos, louder and more prolonged, caused the members of the Garduna to redouble their attention.

" Do you hear? do you hear? they are coming," said the gitano, terrified, endeavouring to drag Dolores away, but the governor's daughter, with a violent and scornful look, thrust her off—

"Be accursed," she said, "thou who hast lied."

At these words, la Chapa again concealed herself near the Giralda, and Dolores, half-mad with despair and fright, ran towards the esplanade.

She had proceeded but a short distance, when four emissaries of the Inquisition rushed from the four angles of the square and snatched her up in their sturdy arms, without its being possible for her to make the least resistance, or even utter a single cry.

After thus possessing themselves of their victim, the men proceeded towards the Guadalquivir, where Enriquez and Frasco were waiting near one of the carriages belonging to the Inquisition. This carriage was especially prepared for a nocturnal expedition; it was a kind of coach; its four wheels covered with thick but soft leather, produced no sound as they rolled over the pavement, and the mules that drew it wore on their feet their night boots of buffalo hide.

At the last signal of the chivatos, Coco and the two guapos left their hiding place, and gliding along the walls of the cathedral, followed in the steps of the ravishers, while the serena followed with stealthy pace. In the meantime, the chivatos, crawling on their hands and knees like serpents, were in advance of the rest, and moved towards the carriage.

Enriquez and Frasco were there in waiting, but, when they heard the officers coming, they advanced a few paces towards them; the chivatos, like accomplished rogues, taking advantage of the moment their attention was distracted, cut the traces and carried off the mules, who seemed as if they had been shod so softly for the very purpose of being stolen. Like true sons of the Garduna, the chivatos began their business by throwing the driver, who rather interfered with their operations, into the Guadalquivir, and all this was done in less time than we have taken to write it.

"There she is," said Enriquez to Frasco, when they drew near the men who had the fainting Dolores in their arms.

"It has been well done," said Frasco, in a brutal tone, "hold your tongue and let us make an end of it."

"We have her now," exclaimed Enriquez, triumphantly.

"Not yet!" cried Manofina, dealing the familiar a vigorous blow with his dagger on the left arm.

Enriquez thus surprised, staggered from the effects of the sudden pain he felt, but he soon regained his courage, and shouting for help, two of the officers of the Inquisition, leaving the governor's daughter with their comrades, ran to assist the familiar.

Frasco had not waited for this, but at the first cry of the wounded man, he rushed towards Manofina! Enriquez on the other hand, furious with pain, and unable to distinguish his enemies in the darkness, fiercely attacked Cuerpo de Hierro, and a desperate struggle ensued.

While this was taking place, Coco was in pursuit of the two officers, who hearing the noise of the strife, ran with all haste to the carriage, and after having placed Dolores within it, they took to their heels without waiting the issue of the combat.

Coco, doubtful whether he should stay to protect the governor's daughter, or assist his comrades, hesitated for a few instants, but his warlike feelings at length got the better of him, and he entered the lists just in time to save Cuerpo de Hierro, who, in spite of his lion-like courage and vast strength, had some trouble in making head against three adversaries, the two officers, and Enriquez ; for the latter, notwithstanding his wound, fought with desperation.   The arrival of the alguazil changed the aspect of affairs.

Thus fighting on, the agents of the Inquisition endeavoured to reach the bridge, where the carriage was standing, and the Gardunas, on their side, redoubled their efforts to force them there, being in that case certain of making short work of them; and, in fact, the officers had no sooner set foot on the bridge of Triana, than they were mortally wounded by the two Gardunas, and thrown into the water.   Enriquez, quite exhausted, had fallen a short distance from the bridge, and Cuerpo de Hierro having come up with him, lifted him in his arms to the top of the parapet, and threw him into the river.

Coco returned to the carriage, imagining that Manofina, being alone with Frasco, would have no trouble in getting rid of him; but in this he was deceived, for Frasco, finding himself alone against the guapo, and seeing well he had an ugly customer in the bandit, threw round his neck one of those murderous weapons, a silken thong with a running knot, in the use of which the Andalusians are so famous.   And it would soon have been all over with Manofina, whose courage and skill were becoming useless, for, suffocating under the pressure of the cord, he was gradually losing his breath and strength.   The poniard dropped from his trembling hand, his red and glaring eyes were covered as with a cloud, and Frasco was in the act of raising his hand to make an end of him, when he was himself struck to the heart, and fell on the ground stark dead.

Culervina had smitten him with her slender Andalusian blade ; and she hastened to loosen the cord which still compressed Manofina's throat, for in spite of his horrid punishment he still was on his legs.

"Bravo! Culervina," he said, grasping the serena's hand, "you are a fine courageous girl, and the master shall reward you."

"Not so; I expect my recompence from you."

"From me!" said the guapo, in surprise; "what is it you want? By the Vierge des Douleurs, I swear I will grant you all you ask!"

"Manofina," she said, at the same time hanging on his arm, with the cunning of her sex, "I ask you to save Don Estevan de Vargas."

"Culervina," cried the guapo, in a tone of vexation, "you ask an impossibility.   And of what moment is his death to you?" he added, with a louring look.

"You ought not to silence those who love so well," replied the serena; "and the governor's daughter will die of grief if you take away her intended husband, as I should have died to-night if you had been killed, dear Manofina."

"I cannot promise you," replied the guapo, much softened, but terribly embarrassed, for he did not like to betray what he called his duty, and he did not wish to displease her he loved.

The serena hung her head, and shed tears.

"Do not weep, my soul," said the guapo, pressing her to his breast, "we will see what we can do."

While this was taking place, Coco and Cuerpo de Hierro had removed the still insensible Dolores from the carriage.

IV.

"What shall we do with this little lady?" said Manofina, going up to Coco.

"Follow me, and look out for squalls;" and Coco, going before Cuerpo de Hierro, walked in the direction of the house of the apostle, situated on the other side of the Guadalquivir, while Manofina and the serena followed at a distance, ready to defend them against any ambush of the Inquisition.

CHAPTER V.

A MONKISH BANQUET.

HE palace of the Grand Inquisitor, Pierre Arbues, was an immense and sumptuous Moorish edifice, formerly inhabited by the King of Seville. After passing through magnificent gardens, filled with the most beautiful flowers and rarest trees, you arrived at an isolated pavilion, formerly occupied as baths, but the voluptuous Arbues had devoted it to a very different purpose.

This pavilion, at a distance from the principal building, almost lost in a mass of foliage, was the spot where the jovial meetings of the Grand Inquisitor and his favourites were usually held. In those days bishops and monks threw aside the restraint of cross and gown, when celebrating their midnight orgies, and gave full rein to their debauchery. The monks reserved for their nightly meetings the exhibition of the feelings forcibly engendered by the habitual constraint of their life—a torrent increased by the obstacles it had met with in its course, and replete with all the filth it had dragged along with it; for want of other food for the devouring lava of their imagination, the monstrous laws of the Inquisition were elaborated—a barbarous code to which the reign of each successive Inquisitor added additional ferocities.

These men had so strong a necessity for devouring emotions that they could only appease their insatiable desire for excitement by blood and butchery. Some among them, we are told, acted honestly in their fanaticism; let the history of the Inquisition be read, and then answer. This monstrous institution, created by the policy of the popes, protected in Spain by the policy of the kings, did not belie the impurity of its source; and the agents of a wicked power were as wicked as it.

It was midnight. A sumptuous table was spread in an elegant room in the solitary pavilion attached to the inquisitorial palace. The ceiling of the apartment was covered with delicate arabesque ornaments, the precious work of the Moors. On the walls richly coloured fresco paintings represented fruits and flowers of every description, imitating nature sufficiently close to make her jealous, and enclosing panels which the artistic taste of the inquisitors had adorned with the most voluptuous scenes from the heathen mythology.

There was Clytie reposing on a bed of flowers, turning her eyes, which glowed with amorous aspirations, towards the sun. Jupiter, that immortal voluptuary, under the form of a swan, was sporting in the waves close by the beauteous Leda, and many others of a like description, all intended to gratify the morbid imaginations of the assembled guests. Rich marble mosaic work formed the flooring of the room, and on a table, in the centre, the choicest fruits, the most exquisite viands, were placed in vases of rock crystal, or vessels of china. The Xeres, Tintarrota, the sweet Malaga wine, the juice of the banana, but lately brought from America, every description of intoxicating wine produced beneath a fiery sky, circulated freely among the guests ; musk-scented bishops, and merry monks, having his eminence, the grand Inquisitor of Seville, for a president.

A wild and somewhat mystical gaiety animated every countenance, and the eyes of Pierre Arbues shone with unusual fire. Their heads were beginning to grow giddy ; but they were still under the control of reason, each knew his proper rank, and a touch of monkish prudery still veiled the freedom of their language.

Arbues was the first to break through this constraint. " Are you aware, brothers," he exclaimed in a voice slightly affected by drink, " that Heaven's gate-keeper, the Pope, is still forging fresh keys to guard more surely the avenues to that delightful kingdom, and to increase our joys here on earth ? The Inquisition is established in Portugal, and soon there will not be the smallest spot on the earth where our domination shall not extend !"

" So much the better," said the Archbishop of Toledo ; " the Inquisition is a mill where the bad grain we crush is changed into glorious Spanish doubloons—"

" And the doubloons into heavenly joys and delicious feasts," said the prior of the Dominicans, with his luxurious face and glowing eyes.

" And so excellently, that it is better to be Inquisitor than Pope ; and the gate-keeper of Paradise, who calls himself our master, is no more, if the case be well considered, than the steward of our private pleasures."

" And then," said a young monk, " a pope is so old ! what is the use of the good things of this world when you can no longer enjoy them ?"

" It would be much better to be a novice in a convent of Dominicans, is not that true, José ?" said the Grand Inquisitor to the young novice.

" It is better to be the humble slave of your eminence," replied the young monk, with feigned humility.

" The Pope sows, and we reap merrily," observed the Archbishop of Toledo ; " and while he and his cardinals are yawning in each other's faces, we are gathering in the fields of Cythcrea the sweetest flowers of love as they spring up in our path."

" I," said the Archbishop of Malaga, who was present at the orgy, " I have no necessity even to stoop to gather them, the superior of the convent of the barefooted Carmelite nuns takes that trouble off my hands, and offers me the first-fruits of the most beautiful flowers in her garden."

"As for me," said the prior, "I like to gather them myself; when my lucky star leads young and pretty penitents to my confessional, they very seldom return as they came; I have no pity on any who are under thirty."

"I give myself much less trouble than that," said the Archbishop of Toledo; "when a woman pleases me, I get the brotherhood of the Garduna to carry her off for me."

"A useful institution, that," said the Grand Inquisitor; "we ought to protect it with all our power, my lords. The very day the society of the Garduna ceases to exist in Spain, we may bid adieu to our pleasures and vengeance; we shall be obliged to take matters into our own hands, and our interests will be sadly compromised."

"Bah!" cried another Inquisitor; "none are equal to the familiars of the holy office for nightly abductions and secret assassinations. A familiar is as silent as death, and he can do everything with impunity for the very word 'Inquisition' is a warrant for all his acts: no one dares to murmur."

"Poor fools," said Pierre Arbues, whispering in the novice's ear, whose deadly paleness formed a strange contrast to his mirth; "poor fools, they are more intoxicated with vanity than with the wine I lavish on them."

"And your eminence is their master in every thing," said the novice, in a low tone: "you can preserve your reason during the orgy, and do in cold blood all they brag of in their drunkenness."

The noise of the conversation prevented these words being heard.

"Enriquez is long before he comes," said the Inquisitor anxiously. "You did not meet him, then, on the Triana bridge, Josè?"

"No," replied the young monk, "I thought it most prudent to leave the business to him; but do not be uneasy, Enriquez is to be trusted."

"What is the subject of your conversation, my lords?" said Pierre Arbues, addressing the bishops of Malaga and Toledo.

"My lord," returned the archbishop, "we were talking of the pretty girls you have in your city of Seville, and I maintain, to the Bishop of Malaga, that the most beautiful among them is Dolores Argoso, the governor's daughter."

Arbues started with surprise.

"Oh! as to her," said the fat prior, "she is as impregnable as a citadel; I have confessed her twice, and I have a strong suspicion she has a touch of heresy in her—she is as controversial as a disciple of Luther."

"What a beautiful heretic she would be to be burned," said the Bishop of Malaga.

"You mean with the flames of love, no doubt?" said the Bishop of Toledo, "she would be a conquest worthy of his eminence."

"Have you no more difficult task to propose than that?" observed Pierre Arbues, with a smile full of vanity.

His eminence hesitates.

"I do not hesitate," replied the Inquisitor, casting a haughty glance over the assembly, "but really, I should be sorry to perform so little for your gratification, fathers."

"No, no! we shall be very well satisfied with that," exclaimed the whole party in chorus.

At this instant, the heavy silk curtain at the end of the apartment was raised, and a familiar went up to the Grand Inquisitor.

"My lord," he said, "Enriquez wishes to be introduced to your eminence."

A triumphant smile lighted up the face of Pierre Arbues.

"My lords, talk of the devil—you shall see the governor's daughter directly," then turning to the familiar, "let Enriquez come in," he said.

The familiar disappeared, and all eyes were directed to the door of the banqueting-room.

"My lord," continued Arbues, addressing the Archbishop of Toledo, "I must entreat you to grant me a hundred days' indulgence for this excellent Enriquez; he is the best servant the Holy Inquisition possesses."

As Arbues left off speaking, the curtain was again raised, and the "excellent Enriquez" entered, pale, bleeding, and dripping wet, but alone, and scarcely able to stand.

"What is the matter?" exclaimed the Inquisitor, in surprise.

"My lord," replied the familiar, in a feeble voice, "all our sbirri (officers) have been killed, the governor's daughter has been carried off, and with great difficulty I saved myself by swimming, to bring you an account of my mission."

Everybody surrounded Enriquez, who then related, in feeble accents, the adventures of the evening, and during his recital the eyes of the Inquisitor sparkled with rage.

"You were all of you cowards alike, then?" he observed, with frightful sarcasm.

"We all did what lay in our power to obey the orders of your eminence," replied Enriquez, timidly.

"And Frasco?" continued Pierre Arbues.

"Dead, my lord! dead, like the rest," answered the familiar, who was ignorant of the flight of the first two sbirri.

"You are a miserable wretch," exclaimed the Inquisitor, in a voice of thunder, "leave my presence, and never let me see you again."

Enriquez, weak from the loss of blood, his unexpected bath in the Guadalquivir, and the emotions he had endured during the evening, could not bear up against this last blow: his limbs failed, and he sank on the ground, in a state of insensibility.

Pierre Arbues rang the bell, and two servants appeared—"Take this man away," he said, coldly. Then turning towards the guests—"take your seats, my lords, and let us finish the evening as we began it."

The monks and the bishops reseated themselves, and the intoxicating liquors were again circulated.

Pierre Arbues was in his heart full of rage, but he appeared replete with mad merriment, and smart and biting words.

"Josè," said Arbues, in the ear of the novice, "this will be a dear evening for the Governor of Seville."

An emotion full of bitter joy crossed the brow of the novice, but the Inquisitor did not understand its meaning.

The orgy lasted until the morning.

CHAPTER VI.

THE HERETIC'S DWELLING.

THE dwelling of the apostle was a small isolated country-house, in the midst of a rural garden, watered by the Guadalquivir. The apostle was one of those preaching monks and confessors, who although they followed the rules of the order to which they belonged, were attached to no religious corporation.

This monk was the same we have already seen at La Chapa's tavern. He had chosen this humble retreat as a place of rest from his labours, and here, on account of its distance from the town, and proximity to the river, it had many a time answered the purpose of a place of refuge for the victims of the Inquisition.

It was the morning after the day, on the evening of which so many events had taken place. Dolores was alone in the chamber which served her for an asylum. Night was coming on, and shrouded every object with its dull hues. Notwithstanding the sharp wind that blew without, Dolores opened the window, and separating the long tresses that shrouded her face, with her white hand, she exposed her bare and burning forehead to its sharp and freezing breath. Deep despair oppressed her soul, and her eyes were swelled with weeping. Vainly in the profundity of her grief had she sought the consolation of prayer; the mortal wound of her soul could not be healed. This young, yet strong-minded girl, whose whole faith rested on the pure principles of the gospel, the simple enthusiast, who wished to find God in the priest, for the priest in her eyes was not man, but a transformed being; this exalted adorer of every ideal perfection, a poetess in love and in religion, could not, without the deepest horror, contemplate the abyss of luxury and hypocrisy in which those who called themselves the ministers of Heaven were plunged.

"What!" she exclaimed with anguish, "are these the representatives of Heaven, the depositaries of the law? why are they not swept out of the temple, as the sellers were of yore? Why are not the flames of the faggots they light turned against themselves, that they may be consumed?"

A scorching and holy anger filled the soul of the young girl, and she looked upwards to the quiet heaven, which remained unmoved at the miseries of the earth, and remembering her weakness, and the terrible power of the Inquisition, she asked herself, with terror, whether Heaven cared for human woes. Her doubts had assumed a tangible shape, and there was but one step to incredulity. Besides, it must be remarked, this age of terror and persecution teemed with sects as numerous as they were absurd; every man wished to create a faith after his own fashion, for no one could be contented with the barbarous creed promulgated by torture and flame.

"Oh, Heaven!" she exclaimed, "why are the crimes of these butchers permitted?"

"To purify the good," said a mild and serious voice beside her; and, turning her head to the side from whence it came, Dolores saw the angelic form of the apostle, as he was called.

"Oh! father," cried the young girl, falling on her knees before him, "father, support me, for I waver, and my terrified soul can believe in naught but evil! Has not the demon possessed himself of the world to drive out true religion?"

"Child," said the monk, placing his hand upon the burning brow of Dolores, "since when has strength yielded to weakness? Is not evil weak, and goodness powerful?"

"Oh! pardon me," exclaimed the maiden, "I have not the strength of a martyr; and it appears to me that happiness ought to be the birthright of mankind."

"Happiness is here," said the monk, placing his hand on his heart.

"No," cried Dolores, in despair; "even that asylum is not inviolable for the Inquisitors."

"Can they repress its pulsations, or accelerate its movements?" replied the monk; "can they banish a cherished image, or drive out the faith of your forefathers? Do you not feel the superhuman power of the soul, that says to thee, 'Go on—fear nothing—love and believe: the body may be oppressed, but the feeling of love within us is imperishable: but the soul never dies!'"

"Oh! thanks, thanks," said Dolores, kissing the hands of the holy man, and covering them with her tears; "thanks for your consolation." The monk meekly withdrew his hands. "Oh!" continued Dolores, "you are humble and strong, and yet believe; I, poor, weak, persecuted woman, ought also to believe. Oh! father, who are you that thus comforts me? Tell me thy name, that I may repeat it in my prayers."

"I am the humble servant of Heaven, and am called John," replied the monk; "invoke Heaven in your prayers, not me. But," he added, "it is growing late; it is time you returned to your father's house. Come, I will be your guide; and if ever you are oppressed, if ever you need assistance, remember this humble dwelling—it is always open to those who mourn."

Dolores looked up to Heaven with resignation.

"I follow you, father," she said; and casting a last glance upon the blessed roof which had sheltered her, she enveloped herself in her mantle, and went out, accompanied by the monk.

They walked for a considerable time side by side, without uttering a word, vague forebodings agitated the mind of the young girl, her forehead, formerly so calm and pure, was oppressed by the storm which had torn from her her crown of happiness. They drew near to the governor's house, and Dolores uttered a cry of joy when she recognised the street in which the palace stood; she redoubled her pace, dragging the monk after her.

"Oh, my father!" she exclaimed, "I shall see you again;" Dolores dared not pronounce the name of Estevan—she advanced. "But why is the lamp that shines each evening in the façade of the palace not lighted?—the door, usually open, resists her efforts! She knocks—no answer—she calls the names of her favourite servants—but no voice is heard in reply to hers. A frightful silence reigns over the house, you might have imagined it to be one of those dwellings in which, during a plague, all the inhabitants had died one after the other, and that it had not yet been opened for fear of contagion. Dolores, overcome, and trembling with terror, redoubled her blows upon the insensible door with her bare knuckles, and the iron nails cruelly wounded her delicate hands.

"Father! father!" she cried in accents of despair—no answer.

The monk guessed the truth, and he drew near to the young girl, ready to offer her consolation, for he felt she would need it.

Dolores looked wildly round her. At the noise she had made several doors were half opened. "My father: what has become of my father?" cried the unhappy girl; but no one answered her.

"It is the daughter of the governor who was arrested this morning, by order of the Grand Inquisitor," said several voices, and the doors were again closed, for they shunned the young girl as if she had the plague.

But Dolores heard the word "Inquisitor," and a horrible light broke in upon her. Her father was in the dungeon of the Inquisition, and as the horrible tribunal takes possession of everything belonging to the suspected party, the governor's house was closed, his property confiscated, and his unhappy daughter's only resource was charity—that charity which, perhaps, would be denied the daughter of a heretic.

Dolores wept no more, no complaint escaped from her lips, her eyes were dry and inflamed, and a bitter smile contracted her pallid lips. She went up to the monk, and took firm hold of the sleeve of his dress, as if she meant to attach herself to him—her last refuge; then, in a short, quick voice, she said, " Father, pray to Heaven that it may have pity on me."

The monk answered her not; in so terrible a moment all words would have been useless; he gently took hold of her arm, which he placed within his own, and, leading her along like a timid child, he took

the road to his dwelling. Dolores did not even turn back to take a parting glance of her home; but she hung down her head, and followed her compassionate guide without a word. They had scarcely walked a dozen steps in the street, when, in the darkness, they run against a man, who, sword in hand, was defending himself against another.

Waking from her lethargy, Dolores uttered a piercing scream, she knew the combatant. " Estevan !"—" Dolores !" they cried at the same instant. Dolores drew Estevan towards her. The struggle for an instant ceased, a young woman, hanging on the arm of the other combatant, who wore the rude dress of a brother of the Garduna, seemed endeavouring to take the poniard from his hand, and by her urgent solicitations begging a favour of him he seemed unwilling to grant.

"I cannot," he said, in a determined but trembling voice; "I cannot, Culervina. I have promised to kill him, and he must die."

While uttering these words they found themselves close to the priest, who, alarmed at the incident, had advanced a few paces. The young woman recognised him, and without letting go of the arm of the man, which she held in her vigorous grasp in spite of all his efforts to disengage himself, she fell at the priest's feet.

"Oh, father!" she cried, "do not let Manofina kill this young man! Have we not had murders enough?"

"The apostle!" cried the bravo, who also recognised him, and he bent humbly before the holy man.

"Manofina," said the priest, for he knew all these men by their names, "Manofina, who has commissioned you to kill this man?"

"The Society of the Garduna, father, to which I belong body and soul. To baptise and to silence is as much a part of my business, as it is a part of yours to confess and preach. Let me do my duty, and not steal the money given to me for this purpose."

"Manofina," said the monk, "do you believe in Heaven?"

The bandit bent his head.

"Certainly," your reverence; "I am a good Catholic, and that is why I wish to act conscientiously. Justice before all things. I have promised to kill him, and he must die."

"I tell you truly, Manofina, your acts are deeds of blood, and Heaven abhors bloodshed, my son."

"But if I give up my trade, father, the Inquisition, when I would no longer serve them, would have me burnt as a heretic, or they would send me out of Spain as they did the poor Moors, who were driven out of Seville by thousands; then what would become of this woman, who belongs to me, and depends on me for a living?"

"What does that signify?" said the serena, affected by the gentle words of the monk; "it is better to die than to live in this manner."

"But my companions," said the bravo; "how can I abandon them?"

"No," said the monk, too much of a philosopher to imagine he could thus in an instant detach this rude man from the habits he had followed during his whole life. "No, you shall not leave the brotherhood of the Garduna; but as a good action excuses many sins, you shall employ yourself for the future in saving the victims of the Inquisition."

"But that would be deception," said the bravo, still imbued with his singular notion of probity, and his chivalrous fidelity to the statutes of his order.

"The motive is everything," replied the monk. "If it is your intention to do what is right, is it not the same thing as doing what is right?"

It was much against his will the monk made use of this Jesuitical argument, to which the bravo listened, not quite convinced.

"But, father," at length he said, "would you absolve me for deceiving my comrades? In that case I would do all your reverence wishes, for you would then be responsible for the safety of my soul, and it could not be in better hands."

"I will bless thee every time you save a victim, and I will absolve you from all the murders you do not commit. There, go in peace, my son; may Heaven direct you!"

The bravo fell on his knees before the monk by the side of the serena, and their heads bent at the same time beneath his united hands as he blessed them both.

"He has betrothed us," said the serena in a whisper, as she rose; and the vagrant Bohemian girl, brought up like a bird in a wood, with no other guide than the instincts of her wild nature, started with a chaste and religious emotion; she had caught a glimpse of Heaven through her love, the consecration of the purest sentiment of the soul.

A few paces off, Estevan and the governor's daughter shared each other's sorrows and tears; the joy of meeting each other had at least brought them this comfort, in the despair which had hitherto consumed their hearts, without the means of communicating it to another. Hope—a melancholy, fugitive, and distant hope—hope, which never abandons love, smiled upon them from their darkened sky.

"See," said the serena, for her woman's instinct had explained all to her, "see, Manofina, how unhappy we should have been, if, instead of meeting with her handsome lover, this poor little senora had stumbled over his corpse."

"Culervina," said the guapo, "it seems as if the voice of the monk had given me a new life, and that I am no longer the same man I was this morning; but how shall I be pardoned for all the blood I have spilled—I see that I must leave the Society of the Garduna?"

"The priest told you that one good action hides many sins. Be easy, then, *mi alma*, his reverence has charge of your soul, and if we leave the Garduna, Heaven, that feeds the brutes, will not neglect two Christian creatures."

The guapo and his companion left the place.

Estevan and Dolores had forgotten everything, that they might weep together.

"Come, my children," said the monk; "to-morrow we will consider about choosing a retreat for my daughter, Dolores."

"Father," said Estevan, "we ought to think of how we might leave this unhappy Spain, which devours its worthiest children."

"Fly, when my father is a prisoner!" exclaimed Dolores. "Estevan, how could you imagine it?"

"But you will destroy yourself fruitlessly," said the young man. "Go alone, Dolores; you can wait for me out of Spain, while I employ my credit and my fortune to save your father."

"Save the living!" said the monk, in a low voice, "when the Inquisition does not even respect the ashes of the dead!"

"Oh! speak not thus, father!" said Estevan, who had noticed his words. "Do not remove all hope from this unhappy girl!"

"I will not leave Spain without my father," said the governor's daughter, resolutely.

"To-morrow, daughter," said the monk, " I will take you to the Carmelite convent."

" Estevan," said Dolores, " be cautious ; the Inquisition has its eyes upon you."

When they arrived at the priest's house, Dolores entered first, but Estevan hesitated, not presuming to cross the threshold.

" Come in, both of you, children," said the Franciscan ; " we will pass the night together in prayer.   Come, for you must depart to-morrow."

Estevan followed in silence, and the door closed behind them.

Nearly eleven years before the time in which the occurrences we have related took place, Cardinal Alphonso Manrique, Archbishop of Seville, was called to the eminent post of Inquisitor General of Castille ; but long before that time the hatred of the Spaniards had been excited against the Holy Office.   Numerous conspiracies had broken out, and many remonstrances had been fruitlessly laid before the Pope and the King of Castille.   The Inquisition covered the land with its scaffolds, depeopled towns, and rendered the country sterile by depriving it of its cultivators ; and a rich chivalrous land, a friend of the arts, of liberty, and of glory, was changed into a vast catacomb, where the sight of the dead terrified the living.   But even at that time some noble Spaniards, with hearts full of vigour, and burning with the love of liberty, boldly protested, at the risk of their lives, against the iniquities of the Inquisition.

Among these heroic defenders of the rights of humanity many noble Castillians were found—men of learning, holy bishops, and even members of the council of Castille.   In this state of affairs the king resorted to a few ineffective measures ; among others he suspended the Grand Inquisitor Deza from his office, and also his friend Lucero, the Inquisitor of Cordova, on account of the horrible cruelties of which they were guilty.

Among the noble Spaniards who were hostile to the Inquisition, young Estevan de Vargas was remarkable for the deep indignation he expressed. He had descended from one of those illustrious Moorish families who, before the conquest of Grenada, had voluntarily embraced Christianity. Young, ardent, and hot-blooded, Estevan possessed a masculine and poetical beauty, which indicated rather an energetic mind than bodily strength ; his bronzed complexion, delicate in the extreme, was of a golden tone, the partial transparency of which scarcely gave you an idea of the rapid circulation of the rich and ardent blood that flowed through the delicate net-work of his veins.   His dark eye, usually mild and calm, would sparkle with fire at the least mental emotion ; his figure was tall, active, and graceful, showing his Moorish descent ; and his shining black hair cast its thick shadow over his pale forehead, and crowned his handsome head, fit to support a golden, or rather a laurel, crown ; for Estevan possessed the poetry that charms, the eloquence that persuades and attracts, and his powerful philosophy was worthy of the master he had followed.

Without belonging to any particular sect, without adopting the doctrines either of Luther or Melancthon, he was regulated in his belief by the pure doctrines of the Gospel.   His father, a member of the council of Castille, in 1502, had assisted in the establishment of a society called the Catholic Congregation, whose object was to oppose the unjust and cruel acts of the unworthy Lucero. The young Vargas, when he became a man, was doomed to struggle against the same abuses, and perhaps greater still. What power must not a man like him possess over a mind like that of Dolores !

Pure and perfect love does not arise in common minds: the love of a strong mind for one possessed only of mediocrity is also not a true love, it becomes then either error or weakness. But the perfect fusion of two souls, whose life is as that of one, whose sufferings are the same, whose wishes and desires resemble each other so much that you would imagine you saw but one existence in two individuals—love like this is only formed in souls resembling each other like sisters, and united by perfect affinity. Such was the love of Dolores and Estevan. Affianced to each other by their parents, they felt that their union depended not on the will of man, but that already, by a tacit and inviolable agreement, their souls were attached to each other, and that even death itself could not divide them.

Dolores had, during the day she passed in the house of the preacher, related to him the history of her life, her pious childhood and youth, and her love for Estevan; and the warm-hearted and indulgent man perhaps looking back to some mysterious and chaste affection of his own, broken by the hands of men or by death, hesitated not to say to the young man—

"Enter with thy betrothed, pure love offends not Heaven; it is a homage rendered to the Omnipotent."

And they entered the humble dwelling, whose white walls were only ornamented with a crucifix.

"Children," said the monk, "thank Heaven for your afflictions; happy are those who pass their days in prayer and sorrow."

"Father," replied the young man, "your words are holy and comforting; but for us youth, full of health and strength, Spanish cavaliers, whose fathers have always been true to the religion they voluntarily embraced, with faith and conviction; can we, without cowardice, support the yoke of an iniquitous power, which sets at nought all divine and human laws ?"

The monk remained for a few instants without answering—he appeared to be in deep thought; at length he said—

"I believe the power of the Inquisition to be an abuse we ought to attack with the sword of the tongue and with argument; with truth, and not with insurrection, that child of anguish and hatred—blind, passionate, and unbridled—always going either too far, or not far enough; like a glass of water thrown upon the flames, instead of subduing them it irritates their fury."

"Yes," said Estevan, "they confine truth behind bolts and bars: and as for logic, the sombre genius of the Inquisition understands all its subtleties, or it overcomes all opposition with the words, ' In the name of Heaven !' and the ignorant people bow their heads, for fear they should commit sacrilege by opposing them."

"The people submit," observed the monk, "but their strength lies in resignation ; if they revolt they do but change masters—they spend their blood and strength for the benefit of their leaders."

" Father," returned Estevan, " if the leaders are honest, the people are happy. Evil arises not from obedience, but from hatred towards those in command."

" Certainly," replied the monk ; " he who is worthy of the command becomes willingly the brother and equal of those who obey him ; he is only superior to them by his intelligence ; he is the pilot that stands at the helm for the safety of the crew."

" Father," interrupted Dolores, " what resemblance is there between a leader who governs either by right or choice, and this iniquitous power that depopulates Spain, and covers it with a funeral pall ?"

" The toleration the king shows to the Inquisition," exclaimed Estevan, " is but the policy of avarice. It is the love of gold that covers the land with scaffolds."

" My son," observed the preacher, " Heaven will enlighten kings as to their true interests, and fill their hearts with compassion. The words of the preachers of the Gospel will at length be heard—many among them will raise their voices in defiance of death ; trust in them, my son, the force of conviction is greater than that of the sword."

" Are you a follower of that illustrious reformer, Luther ?" said Estevan.

" I am a Christian," replied the monk, " and I look upon all contro- versy as sacrilegious."

In discussions of this nature the night passed away ; and rapidly did the blood circulate through the veins of the young girl, who at that moment would joyfully have suffered martyrdom, if her death could have saved her brethren, or restored peace and liberty to Spain. As the morning approached, a dull light mingled with the clear brightness of the lamp that burned in the chamber. The matin-bell of the chapel was heard, and the two lovers repeated the Angelus along with the monk. It was daybreak.

" Children," said the preacher, " we must bid each other adieu. I must lead this maiden to a cloister, that she may there await the will of Heaven ; as to you, young man, you are acquainted with my retreat, and I say to you as I said to your intended bride, it is always open to those who weep."

Dolores looked up with sad resignation ; Estevan spoke not, but his pale features betrayed the struggles within his breast—he pressed fondly the hand of his affianced, and stretched out his other hand to the monk, who looked on them with tender compassion, and then rushed out of the room, pronouncing with emphasis the single word—" Courage !"

The monk left the room for a few minutes ; when he returned, he had tied on his sandals, and his right hand rested on an oaken stick.

Dolores was kneeling before the crucifix. At the approach of the monk she turned her head towards him, and seeing he was ready to start, she rose suddenly, and suppressing the painful sigh with which her bosom heaved, she said—

" Father, I am ready to follow you."

CHAPTER VII.

MANOFINA.

HE governor's daughter is still under the guardianship of her holy conductor. Let us return to Manofina, who was left by us under the impression of a sudden conversion.

The bravo and his companion slowly retraced their steps towards the palace of the Garduna; neither of them uttered a word, but, as if for the purpose of confirming himself in the resolution he had taken, Manofina at intervals pressed the arm of his serena fervently, and in this manner they reached the ruins that formed the avenue leading to the strange dwelling of Mandamiento.

A feeble light illumined the interior of the large chamber, which at this time was nearly deserted; none of the members of the fraternity had as yet returned from their nocturnal pursuits, the master alone was in waiting, seated on a broken column, and counting with a greedy eye a handfull of doubloons; here and there a few old women had spread their aprons on the ground, and slept soundly, stretched out on their scanty mattresses.

Roused by the noise made by the young couple as they advanced in the gloom, the master suddenly raised his head, and seeing the bravo, exclaimed, in a joyful tone—

"Ah! is it you, Manofina? Always the first when needed—Don Estevan de Vargas——"

"Is as well as you or I," replied the guapo, in melancholy accents.

"By St. James!" said Mandamiento, "some sorcerer has broken the blade of thy poniard in the scabbard, my fine fellow, or else Don Estevan possesses a talisman that protects him against steel."

"Neither one nor the other, master; I have come to tell you I grow weary of murder, and that I no longer belong to your fraternity. Here is the money that was given to me;" and he threw a purse at the feet of the enraged Mandamiento.

"A thousand demons!" cried the master. "Are you speaking, Manofina, or is it the evil spirit that has taken thy form to deceive me and insult you?"

" It is I myself, in flesh and blood, master," replied the guapo; "I, who have come to take leave of you, and thank you for the especial protection you have honoured me with."

Mandamiento knit his brows, and turned towards the serena, who stood behind the bravo, with downcast looks, and in a humble attitude.

" And you, Culervina," said the master, " do you also wish to renounce the pleasures and emoluments of the trade, to follow this madman, who has no other bread to offer you than the filthy mess the monks distribute ?"

" I renounce them," said the young woman, drawing nearer to her lover.

" A pair of fools !" muttered the master; but Manofina made no answer.

Mandamiento rose suddenly from his stone seat, and paced the room rapidly, uttering at the same time hurried and unintelligible ejaculations. It was the hour when the members of the brotherhood usually returned : they came to acquaint their chief with the result of their different missions. The room was gradually filled with people, but the master, completely absorbed in thought, had neither noticed nor spoken to any one.

At length the meeting was complete; no one had to arrive, with the exception of a few chivatos, who were behind their time—people of little consequence; all the principal men of the order were assembled, and perceiving that Mandamiento, absorbed in his own thoughts, took no more notice of them than if they belonged to the other world, Cuerpo de Hierro took upon himself the task of approaching the chief, and, plucking him gently by the sleeve—

" Master," said he, " all your boys have done your bidding."

" Not all," cried the master, looking sullenly at Manofina, who stood apart from the rest, along with his serena.

All eyes were directed to the apostate guapo, and Manofina looked calmly at his ancient companions, but without saying a word.

" What is that you said ?" exclaimed the astonished group; " is it possible, master ?"

" Yes," replied Mandamiento, in a ridiculously solemn voice; " a garduno has disobeyed orders, and the society loses at one blow two of its bravest supporters; but their cowardly desertion will bring greater evils along with it. Yes," continued the master, pointing at Manofina and his companion, who appeared unmoved, " the order loses in them two of its best children; but it loses more than that—it loses its reputation for probity, the hitherto unblemished name acquired by long and perilous services. What will the noble lords say ?—what the great ladies ? But more than all, what will the clergy think ?—our best customers. What will the Dominicans say, who have filled our coffers with doubloons ? We shall be looked upon through all the kingdom of Andalusia as miserable rogues, who take money for assassination and neglect our duty. They will compare us to the alguazils, who are paid to arrest robbers, and who take up none but honest men ; or those cheating monks who are paid ten times over for saying a mass which they only half perform. Only consider, brothers," continued the master, growing more animated at the sound of his own voice, "only consider the rage of the Grand Inquisitor, when he knows that what he ordered has not been done. And my lord the archbishop, will he not also say that we are cowards and thieves? And then we shall lose the protection of Don Pedro Peladeras y Martinez y Cabrera, the protector of our order and the jester of our noble lord and king Don Carlos, whom may Heaven preserve! Oh! Manofina, Manofina! consider within yourself, and make amends for a moment of weakness."

The assembly listened to this strange harangue with a stupified look. As soon as Mandamiento had left off speaking, several of the hypocritical old men approached Manofina, and said to him—

"Brother, you surely don't mean to abandon us?"

"It is done," said the bravo, firmly.

On the other hand, two of the coberteras, the oldest and most repulsive, went up to the serena, and in coaxing tones endeavoured to induce her to return to her late vocation.

"It is useless," she answered; "what is said, is said, and we do not change."

"What! Manofina a cheat?" cried a guapo, who had been promoted the evening before.

"Manofina is not a cheat," replied the bravo; "he has returned the money he had received; and he declares before you all that he has failed, that he dislikes the trade, and relinquishes all its titles and privileges."

Manofina spoke in a mild tone; he was no longer the turbulent man of the previous evening, eager for perilous and horrible deeds—he was still a strong and courageous man, converted by the words of the monk, still fond of danger and peril, but not without an object in view; all his warlike ardour was directed now against the oppressors of the weak— against the sbirri of the Inquisition.

"To the justice with him!" exclaimed the new-made guapo.

"Brother," said the master, in a severe tone, "the brotherhood of the Garduna has never given up its children to the magistrates of Seville, not even the most guilty. If they are weak, cowardly, or unskilful, they are degraded and dismissed; if they are traitors, they are stabbed; but it never gives them up to the vengeance of the beak."

"Master," said Manofina, "the brotherhood never informs against its children, and its children never betray it; it will have nothing to fear from me."

"My son," replied the master, much affected, "why do you wish to leave us? Have you any complaint against me? You have still time to repair your fault"

"Never!" said Manofina, resolutely.

"Do you know," returned Mandamiento, irritated, "do you know that every faithless member deserves punishment?"

"Every faithless member is degraded; degrade me, therefore, and make an end of it."

"You ought to know that in certain cases they are dispatched," replied Mandamiento, severely.

"Traitors only are served in that manner, and I am no traitor."

"But——"

"But you may fear I shall become one, you mean to say, and then I shall be put out of the way. Is that not it?" added the bravo, with a look of defiance. "Well, I advise the man who undertakes the job to confess himself beforehand; for, by the beard of the king, he will stand in need of absolution! My poniard shall not for the future be at the command of any one who requires its services, but it will be always ready to defend its owner."

The defiance of Manofina affected the self-love of several of the brethren, and their hands flew to their daggers. The serena, who had noticed this movement, clenched convulsively the handle of her little Andalusian stiletto.

The guapo who had been installed the previous evening approached Manofina with a sneering expression of countenance, and said—

"I never thought you were cowardly, Manofina," and he smiled disdainfully.

"What are you about there?" said the master. "Are you not aware no one is allowed to whisper at our solemn meetings?"

"I said to Manofina," replied the newly-promoted brother, "it is a pity he should have become a coward; for I maintain it was fear prevented his performance of his duty."

The words were scarcely out of his mouth when the new-made brother rolled at Mandamiento's feet—carried away, as if with a whirlwind, by a sturdy cuff on the ear from the vigorous hand of Manofina. The next instant twenty poniards gleamed over Manofina's head; but the latter, without disconcerting himself, rolled his cloak round his left arm, grasped his poniard in his right, and, placing himself in an attitude of defence, steadily awaited the attack of his assailants. The serena, when she noticed this, also rolled her mantilla round her left arm, and placing herself back to back with the bravo, she waited, with raised poniard, the attempt of those who might be induced to attack her lover in the rear. No one dared to move.

" Well," observed Manofina, " is that all ?"

" Come on, you race of cowards !" cried Culervina, her eyes sparkling like those of a tigress ; " come on, and see if we have forgotten how to baptise ?"

Mandamiento remained passive.

The guapo, who had been already overthrown, arose as furious as a wounded jackal, and rushed at Manofina ; but to the great disappointment of the assembly he again rolled on the earth ; for Manofina, shrouding his face with his left arm, had at the same instant applied a vigorous kick to his opponent, and stretched him on the ground—but the rest of the assembly stirred not.

" Senores, you are a pack of cowards !" cried Manofina ; " you will oblige me to make an end of this young pullet, who has more spirit than experience."

" Manofina," at length the master said, " this young pullet, as you call him, is entitled to satisfaction, and you are too brave to refuse it to him."

" I am ready to give him every kind of satisfaction, but in a regular manner, one to one."

" Culervina will help you," said the others, with a sneer.

" Culervina will remain as still as death," replied the bravo ; " you do the same, and leave us, this young man and myself, to settle our affairs peaceably."

" Order, children," said Mandamiento ; " let every poniard be placed in its scabbard ; and as for you, Senor Garabatillo," he added, turning to the young garduno who acted as his page, " go and keep watch, and at the least sign of the approach of a trap, croak like a frog ;" and the messenger departed.

The men and women formed themselves into a large circle in the hall of the Garduna, and the guapo and Manofina, both armed with their long Albacete knives, advanced to the centre of the living circle ; but before the combat began the two adversaries scrupulously compared their arms, to ascertain if they were alike ; they were found to be exactly of the same length, and their slender blades were precisely of the same width. The examination over, the two combatants rolled their cloaks round the left arm, to answer the purpose of a buckler, and then fiercely stood opposite to each other. Thus placed, they waited the signal ; but the new-made guapo, like a young game-cock whose spurs have just sprouted, first cried out—

"*Ande usted*—now come on !"

At this cry the two men rushed at each other, stooping, drawing back, and writhing their supple forms like a couple of snakes. The rapid movements of the young guapo in a short time rendered him breathless ; and Manofina, more calm and experienced, had the decided advantage. The young guapo, blinded by his passion, and furious at pursuing a shadow that constantly escaped him, rushed in desperation at the well-skilled Manofina, neglecting his own defence while making the attack, and more than twenty times did he expose his breast to the murderous weapon.

Culervina, with sparkling eye and heaving chest, watched the fearful struggle that held every soul in suspense. Some of those present were praying inwardly for the young bravo, whom they expected to see stretched lifeless on the ground.

The young garduno, already much fatigued, had made himself breathless by his imprudent method of fighting. Twenty times the poniard of Manofina had grazed his bosom; but Manofina, who had no wish to kill him, took advantage of the moment when his adversary rushed at him with his arm in a horizontal position—the knife directed against his breast—and suddenly raising the left arm, with a violent and unexpected blow he sent the young man's Albacete knife rolling towards the master's feet.

"Bravo! bravo!" they cried on all sides. "Bravo, Manofina! you are still worthy to be one of us."

"I thank you, brethren," replied the serena's lover, "I thank you; but your approbation is quite sufficient."

"You are really a brave fellow, Manofina," said the conquered man, holding out his hand. "No malice, brother."

Manofina cordially grasped the proffered hand; then approaching Mandamiento, he said—

"Now, master, let us finish the ceremony, that I may be free."

Mandamiento perceiving that all attempts to alter the determination of the guapo would be useless, drew forth his poniard, placed the point against the ground, and bending the blade sharply, he broke it in half, and gave the broken pieces to Manofina, who gave him his own poniard in return. By this exchange the bravo was for ever degraded, and rendered unworthy to take a part in the exploits of the Garduna, or share in its glory.

Mandamiento then took the guapo by the hand, and placed him before an image of the Virgin, when Manofina, kneeling, swore never to betray the Garduna, or any of the brothers of the order, never to become a member of the police to the detriment of the Garduna, and never to draw his poniard against any of them, excepting in legitimate defence.

The ridiculous ceremony over, the bravo took his companion by the arm, and casting a farewell glance on his old comrades, he left the den of the Garduna never again to enter it.

"Brothers," said the master, as soon as Manofina had disappeared, "let us have nine days' prayers offered up to Our Lady, that she may deign to send us a worthy successor to the poor misguided lad who has just left us."

CHAPTER VIII.

THE INQUISITOR'S FAVOURITE.

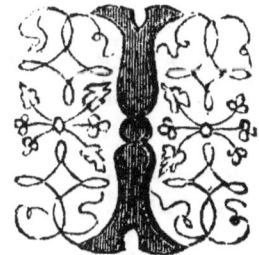T was the day after the feast, about ten o'clock in the morning; the Inquisitor had just risen—his face bore the traces of the excesses of the previous evening, and of that uneasy sleep that wears out the strength, instead of repairing it; the features of Father Arbues were of a livid paleness.

The agitation of an ungratified passion, and deep anger against the agents of his crimes, were added to the nervous excitement produced by intemperance. Enriquez had in the highest degree excited his resentment, for the wild passion the Inquisitor felt for Dolores rose above all the obstacles that had been thrown in the way of his projects.

The bilious tint of Pierre Arbues was every now and then marked with violet-coloured spots, his large dark blue eyes had become as yellow as that of a tiger, and his aquiline profile, violently contracted, gave him a peculiarly ferocious look. He went up to a pan of burning coal that stood in the middle of the room, and warmed his stiffened fingers in its friendly heat; he was cold, the violence of his sensations had concentrated all his vital heat in his brain.

" Dolores !" he exclaimed, " Dolores !"

His excited imagination represented to him, as in a magic mirror, the superhuman beauty of the governor's daughter; he started from his seat and clenched his teeth in a fit of overpowering frenzy.

" How beautiful she looks," continued the Inquisitor, still haunted by the image of the young girl; how beautiful in the midst of her terror! To have seen her thus in my own house, to have had her in my power, and so it might have been but for the cowardice of Enriquez—the vile slave, he knows how to flatter, not to serve; the accursed race that lick the dust from off our sandals, and fly from danger when we need their help. But," he continued, raising his head proudly, " am I not master here, and can I not obtain by force that which evades our art ?" And going up to the silk curtain that separated the room from an anti-chamber, where the familiars of the Holy Office were in attendance, he ordered his secretary to be called.

The secretary came; he was a young man, of a poor but noble family, who to escape from misery and persecution had entered the service of his eminence. Was not everything at the disposal of the Inquisition ?

" Don Philippe," said the Inquisitor, " has the Governor of Seville been arrested during the night, and taken to the prisons of the Holy Office?"

Don Philippe inclined his head.

"My lord, the orders of your grace have been executed."

The eyes of the Inquisitor sparkled with joy.

"Pray desire them to send Don José to me;" and the secretary left the room.

The Inquisitor began to pace the chamber.

"At least," said he, "I can avenge myself on her; and then I hope those accursed gitanos I protect will have performed their task better than my familiars: the children of the Garduna seldom fail in what they undertake, and this Estevan, I hate, will no longer exist—at least I shall have dragged my hated rival from Dolores."

While he thus spoke the pale face of José was seen at the door of the room, and at sight of him the physiognomy of the Inquisitor became singularly softened.

"Come in, José," he said, "I am always glad of your company."

"My lord has passed a bad night?" asked the favourite, affectionately.

"Yes, I have slept badly, José; I have had a very fatiguing and uncomfortable night."

"My lord, there is in the palace a poor man, who has also slept badly, wounded, as he has been, both in body and mind, in the service of your eminence." The eyes of Pierre Arbues sparkled with rage, but José continued, without being disconcerted. "This man, my lord, nearly lost his life in the service of your eminence, and when he returned to you, bruised and bleeding, your eminence drove him out as if he had been an unclean beast, and since then you have refused to listen to his explanation."

"José," exclaimed the Inquisitor, in an angry tone, "do you not know that if any other than you had dared to intercede for Enriquez——"

"Your eminence would have listened to him as you have listened to me," continued the favourite, calmly; "for your eminence is, above all things, just, and your soul reproaches you for your cruelty towards poor Enriquez."

"A traitor!" muttered Arbues.

"A servant who is ready to die for you, my lord—a brave, faithful servant, of whom you stand in need. Whom do you now intend to make Governor of Seville?"

"By the Pope's slipper, Master José, you are witty; I know not which of us two is most mad—you, a young headstrong fellow, for addressing such nonsense to me; or I, Grand Inquisitor of Seville, for listening to you."

"My lord," continued José, "I will prove to you in a few minutes that we are both of us very sensible people."

"I am rather curious to know how you will prove that?"

"Nothing more easy, my lord. You deprived our noble city of Seville of her much-honoured and very honourable governor, Count Manuel Argoso; the city, therefore, is without a mentor, and your eminence without an ally. In these heretical times, my lord, an ally is indispensable."

"What are you aiming at?" said the Inquisitor, who began to listen more complacently.

"I wish to prove to you, my lord, that the best ally the Inquisitor can possess is the governor of the town; and it is particularly necessary he should be a creature of your eminence. Well, then, where will you find a more devoted man than this poor Enriquez, who, in the mere act of carrying off a young girl, suffered two or three baptisms, as those accursed Bohemians call them, and the most complete ducking it is possible to imagine?"

Pierre Arbues smiled; the favorite's influence had cooled his feverish blood. "Enriquez, governor of Seville," he exclaimed with a sudden burst of merriment; "but are you not aware, José, he is a man of no consequence?"

"The greater will be your eminence's power in making him of consequence," replied José, without being disconcerted.

A burst of laughter, but neither infectious nor in sympathy with anything. An Inquisitor's laugh was the only answer to this sally.

José persevered with all the cunning perseverance of a spoiled child. "Shall I call poor Enriquez, my lord, that he may justify himself, and beg to be restored to your good graces?"

"He is very sorry, then, for the failure of his expedition?"

"He is perfectly contrite, my lord."

"It is perfectly true," said Arbues, "a man who has received three baptisms, and is perfectly contrite, deserves absolution. Go, then, and seek Enriquez, my little José."

The novice kissed the hand of the Inquisitor with feverish haste; but any one who had remarked his features as he bent over the hand of Pierre Arbues, would have imagined from the expression of hatred in his looks that he would have willingly torn his master's hand with his teeth, instead of covering it with a hypocritical kiss. José left the room.

"After all," said the Inquisitor to himself, "the idea of this boy is not so bad. Enriquez, governor of Seville, raised by me and supported by me alone, would become the docile instrument of my will, the lictor to whom I might say 'strike,' and he would strike. Yes, José is right, and he has shown much sense." As he concluded, the favourite entered, followed by Enriquez.

The familiar was still pale, and his wounded head and arm were enveloped in bandages; while his hypocritical look gave to his meagre and harassed features a still more sickly and suffering appearance.

When he saw him, the Inquisitor's brow again reddened, the disgraced man knelt down, and by his looks appeared to beg to be permitted to kiss his eminence's hand. Pierre Arbues looked at his favourite: be indulgent, said José's looks.

"I pardon you, Enriquez," observed the Grand Inquisitor; "but you must thank Don José, who has pleaded for you better than an advocate: and now give me a detailed account of the nocturnal expedition in which you received these wounds."

Enriquez did not allow himself to be asked twice, and he related to his eminence what we already know of the abduction of Dolores, not forgetting to attribute to himself all the honour of the blows that were given and received; in fact, he only took what belonged to the dead—it was an inheritance, and not a robbery.

When he had concluded, the Inquisitor, somewhat softened, or rather entirely subdued with respect to him, said to him in a tone full of kindness and patronage :—" Enriquez, I believe you to be faithful, and, although you have been unsuccessful in this enterprise, I hope that for the future your efforts and care in the service of Heaven will make up for this check, and to prove to you I have no trace of resentment left, and that, on the contrary, I look upon you as my most devoted servant, I am about to write to the King to beg that the office of governor of Seville may be bestowed on you."

" Is the Count Argoso dead ?" asked Enriquez with a mingled expression of surprise and joy.

" Much the same," muttered José between his teeth; " he is in the dungeons of the Inquisition."

" My lord," said a familiar of the Holy Office, raising the corner of the curtain, " Master Mandamiento wishes to speak to your eminence."

" Estevan is dead," thought the Inquisitor. " Let the master of the Garduna enter," he said; and Mandamiento was introduced. He remained standing in the presence of the Inquisitor; for this untutored man had such a strange and fanatical notion of the prerogatives of his station, that he imagined he was speaking to an equal.

Enriquez made a sign to Mandamiento to take off his cap. The master only answered him with a scornful look; the Inquisitor smiled, and turned towards the garduno.

" Well, it is all over, I suppose ?"

" Nothing has been accomplished," said Mandamiento with a sorrowful look.

" What of Estevan de Vargas ?"

" Estevan de Vargas is at liberty; not a hair of his head is injured. For the first time since its establishment, the Garduna has found a traitor in its bosom, and this traitor was one of its best men," continued Mandamiento with a comical expression of sorrow. He lamented the defection of Manofina, as a good father of a family would weep over the errors of a dear and only son.

" By Satan !" cried the Inquisitor, stamping with rage; " I fail in every way in this case. What is the traitor's name ?" he said sharply.

" I have sworn not to divulge it, my lord, and the name signifies little to your beatitude. I have merely come to return the money advanced to ————, the man who was charged with the undertaking ;" and with the most scrupulous honesty he laid on the table the gold he had received for the assassination of Don Estevan.

" Is there no one among you gitanos who will undertake the business ?" asked the Inquisitor.

" Oh, we are not without brave and faithful brethren, and I dare promise you that for the future——; but then we have lost all trace of our man, and must have a little time."

" Let it be so," replied the Inquisitor, " if you promise me that Don

Estevan shall not escape you. Take your money again, Mandamiento, it is only to bind the bargain; the more difficult the case is, the greater shall be the recompense, my hero."

"Be it so," said the bandit, again taking up the pieces of gold, "within eight days from this time, my lord, I can promise your reverence that the young man shall have received a baptism from the hand of a master."

"Amen!" said José, and he left the room.

"Cannot you tell me, Mandamiento," asked Arbues, "where the Governor of Seville's daughter has taken refuge? If you can take her, master," he continued, "it will be a capture for which I will be prodigal of my gold; try to discover this young girl, and bring her to me."

"Safe and sound," said the bandit, coolly.

"By Heaven!" cried the Inquisitor, who swore indifferently by things holy and unholy, "by Heaven, yes! let not a hair of her head be hurt; do you hear, let her not even be terrified. Have you no women among you who can take charge of that? Let some one of them find out where this young girl is; she will suspect nothing in one of her own sex—let her employ her cunning; but you know how all this is to be done."

"Ah!" thought Mandamiento, "the serena—she was quick and cunning. My lord," he continued aloud, "it shall be attempted, but I promise nothing—it is more difficult than would be imagined."

VII.

"My lord," said Enriquez, in a whisper, "I will discover her myself: shall I not soon be Governor of Seville?"

Arbues bade the garduno go, and this strange man left the room, with his head erect, and a bold look, for he had a lofty idea of his own importance, and this mad notion was still more increased by the singular life he led, while the naturally proud and poetical spirit that pervades the Spanish character, impressed on all the looks and actions of Mandamiento something wildly solemn, but quite indescribable.

When he had left the room, Arbues shrugged his shoulders—

"To come in contact with such as him," he muttered, "and all through the fault of the Church's militia. If the familiars were sufficiently zealous, should we have any need of these Bohemians?"

"My lord," said Enriquez, "if these Bohemians were not in our service, they would fight against us."

"Perhaps that is true," said the Inquisitor; and the familiar, again restored to favour, continued his conversation with Arbues.

Scarcely had Senor Mandamiento gone the distance of a few paces in the street, when he felt himself plucked by the sleeve of his coat. The master turned, and was not a little surprised to find it was the Inquisitor's favourite who had arrested his progress.

"Has his beatitude forgotten anything?" said the Bohemian.

"His beatitude has forgotten to tell you that it is my will that Don Estevan should not die," replied José.

"We must remind him of it," said Mandamiento.

"So long as you are informed of it, it is all you need require," observed the novice.

"His lordship has given me earnest to poniard Don Estevan, and I know of nothing that can prevent my performing his bidding."

"Except my will," said Don José, authoritatively, "and it is my will that Don Estevan should not die, understand me well, Mandamiento; I will return the earnest money to my lord—be easy on that point, and go."

The master was well acquainted with José's power over the Inquisitor, and the resolute tone of the novice made him uncertain how he ought to act—should he offend the master, or the favourite? He reflected an instant, and then turning towards the young monk, who interrogated him by his looks, he said—

"Your reverence, happen what may, you shall be obeyed."

A courtier could not have done it better.

"It is well," said José, "whatever may happen, appeal to me;" and, having placed a well-filled purse in the hands of the garduno, the favourite disappeared at the corner of a street.

"This is a gift," thought Mandamiento, as he contemplated the rich present the young monk had bestowed upon him, "nothing can be more properly gained than what is given to you; I may therefore keep it," and the master of the Garduna withdrew, humming one of those Spanish airs which the gitanos of Andalusia sing even at the present day.

CHAPTER IX.

THE MONK'S VOW.

 SHORT distance from Seville, on a smiling hill whose base is bathed by the Guadalquivir, stood a convent of Dominicans, a vast and sumptuous edifice, built in the midst of an oasis, surrounded by all that is rich and varied in nature, and furnished in the interior with every elegance and comfort, for the purpose no doubt of rendering the self-denial and renunciation of the world less difficult to the sons of Dominic and Gusman.

This convent, or rather palace, formerly the abode of a Moorish prince, served as an asylum for some thirty monks intended to supply the tribunals of the Inquisition. Many among them had figured in the high office of Provincial Inquisitor, and all were remarkable for their pitiless zeal in the extermination of heresy; Arbues himself was particularly attached to this holy asylum, where he frequently came to rest himself from his arduous duties. On this day an important affair had called him to the blissful abode; a gorgeous ceremony was in preparation, at which the presence of the Inquisitor was necessary to add to its solemnity.

It was two months after the disappearance of the governor's daughter. The passion of Pierre Arbues, although not extinguished, allowed a few intervals of rest to his despotic soul, and the piquant pleasures of domination softened, for an instant, the pangs of his unbridled lust.

Besides, Dolores was not the only being in whom the Inquisitor was interested. On this day, José, his favourite, was to take the vows at the Dominican convent, and the friendship of Pierre Arbues for this young man was sufficiently powerful to divert his attention from his ardent passion.

On this solemn day, the convent had been in a bustle from early morning, and the chapel, a vast rotunda, which had preserved in the midst of its Christian ornaments the marks of its Moorish origin, had been decorated with garlands and flowers. Notre-Dame-du-Rosaire the especial patroness of the Dominicans, was dressed in her holiday clothes, silk and velvet concealed her marble form, and this modest queen of angels displayed her diamonds and pearls like an earthly sovereign.

The white marble of the columns disappeared under a tissue of roses, innumerable wax candles blazed on the altar, and from the enervating odour of perfumes, the mythological and fabulous ornaments of the colonnade, and the profusion of flowers that filled the building, you might have said it was a temple of the ancient goddess Venus, changed suddenly into a Christian chapel; only in the place of the Pagan divinity, the image of the Virgin Mary was placed, and on one side of the nave, the statue of the dismal patron of the Dominicans, with his stern features, called solemn thoughts to your mind to which the smiling aspect of the place would otherwise with difficulty have given birth.

On the right, in the abside, a seat covered with velvet, and surmounted by an elegant canopy had been prepared for the Grand Inquisitor; on his right, on a seat rather below his own, the prior of the convent, who usually occupied the higher place, was to sit, for on this occasion he was obliged to conform to the laws of the hierarchy.

About nine o'clock, deep and solemn strains of vocal music resounded through the vaulted chapel, already filled with numerous visitors, who had been invited, chiefly persons of title.

The monks, preceded by a banner, advanced slowly in two ranks, singing the *Gloria in Excelsis*, each carrying a lighted taper in his hand. Their sombre features concealed but badly, beneath their wild asceticism, the passions of this world; this long procession of men clothed in the insignia of the tomb (black and white) had something so melancholy in its appearance, that it froze you with fear. The prior, dressed in his episcopal garments, closed the procession.

The hymns being concluded, the monks stood still and faced each other, and the prior passed between their ranks: two monks, who acted as deacons, followed him; they accompanied the novice, who was dressed in the rich and elegant costume of a Spanish nobleman. The whole four proceeded to kneel in the centre of the abside, on velvet cushions which had been prepared for them, and a Spanish nobleman acted as father to Don José.

Arbues had already taken possession of the seat reserved for him.

After the gospel had been read, the sermon, usual on such occasions, followed; it was full of mysticism relating to the heavenly nature of a conventual life, making no appeal either to the heart or the imagination, but always tending to the object the court of Rome had in view—to crush, for the purpose dominating.

The auditory were delighted with the sermon, but the preacher's eloquence could not prevent the ladies who were present ogling the young novice in the most saintly manner, and admiring his graceful form and handsome features.

José, nevertheless, was extremely pale, and his dark eye had a strange expression, while sombre flashes of pleasure crossed his features.

When the mass had concluded, the prior approached the novice—

"What came you here to seek?" he demanded.

"The salvation of my soul," replied José.

"Do you expect to find it among the pomps of the world?"

"Well, I renounce the pomps of the world."

"It is not enough; you must renounce the flesh and your own will."

" I will take the vow of chastity, and I will be humble and submissive towards those who will point out to me the road to heaven."

" Proceed," said the prior.

Two monks took hold of the novice, and led him behind the altar to a place prepared for his reception. It was a dark chamber lighted by a sepulchral lamp suspended from the centre: on the ground covered with black cloth was a coffin, over which a pall was thrown as if about to be deposited in the grave, round this four white wax candles were burning. On the lid of the coffin a death's head, placed above two cross bones, grinned, and displayed a double row of teeth as white as ivory. Above, fixed in the earth by their staves, the large silver cross, and the manga (a kind of flag carried at funerals), appeared like two ill-omened standards. Near the extremity of the cavern, close by a prie-dieu surmounted by a leaden crucifix, was seen a table covered with black cloth, where the new garments intended for the novice were placed. Finally, at the other extremity, and facing the prie-dieu, a large plate of polished metal fixed in the wall, reflected and multiplied all these dismal objects. The chamber was called the Cave of Salvation, and there the novice was left alone.

He took off his worldly garments, and clothed himself in the garb of the Dominicans, a white tunic and a black scapulary, a dismal costume like the livery of death ; he then removed his cap decorated with feathers, never for the future to have any other head-dress excepting his shaven crown, and in place of the gilded belt that supported his sword, he girded his loins with a cord, the symbol of poverty, and, in the last place, he took off his rich boots, and put on a pair of sandals, which he was for the future to wear constantly.

Half an hour had passed. The hand of the novice trembled as if he had the ague, his pulsation was hurried and unequal, a cold perspiration ran down his pale and smooth cheeks, he kneeled before the crucifix, and prayed in bitter and melancholy accents. Heart-rending sobs issued from his breast, and he murmured some unintelligible words, while a name he alone could comprehend returned constantly to his lips.

During this time the organ filled the chapel with its noble harmony. The chant of the monks arose in vibrating and metallic sounds : the nerves of the young novice, already excited by his long fast, were immoderately exalted, and the chanting of men, and the sound of the organ, resembling the voice of some giant of the other world, assumed in his idea a strange and fantastic character. Instead of holy thoughts, infernal ideas filled his brain, the hymns appeared to him a tissue of horrible irony, instead of flowers, incense and light, he saw nothing but blood and scaffolds, and the voice of the monks resembled the frightful laughter of demons, coolly assisting at the sacrifice of the human race.

The novice imagined he felt a fiery hand placed on his own, and a sharp mocking infernal voice exclaimed, in the midst of the horrible clang —" Come !" and at the same time yielding, in spite of himself, to the ascendancy of his invisible conductor, without even having the trouble of raising himself to walk, José felt himself hurled swiftly from abyss to abyss through a sultry atmosphere, and in the midst of confused sounds, until he reached an immeasurable depth.

There he stopped, he was in the bowels of the earth, and deep night enveloped him in her heavy mantle of darkness. His respiration became rapid, painful, and interrupted, and he seemed as if he were enclosed living in the tomb. But at that moment a door opened before him, and disclosed a strange spectacle. It was an immense scorching and frightful place, from whence an infectious flame issued. Strange and hideous monsters flew heavily by in the space above the dark vapours of the flame, supported on large membraneous wings, resembling black and horny parchment. These monsters uttered cries of sinister and ferocious joy, they laughed and grinned like demons; then they repeated the chorus in a dismal, wearisome, and rattling voice.

" See, there they are! there they are!"

José began to gaze upon them.

Innumerable legions of monks pressed forward to the entrance of this vast Pandemonium, he saw them pass one after the other, and as fast as they arrived they cast off their previous form, and by the ruddy light of the infernal flames he saw them assume the most hideous and strange shapes, and yet, in spite of this transformation, they preserved the desires, inclinations, and intelligence of man, and were obliged to follow the instincts of the unclean being in whose form they were clothed; or else they assumed, at the same time, the shape of two animals of opposite instincts, subjected to the wants of their contrary natures, and feeling in this eternal contradiction horrible sufferings and desires it was impossible to gratify.

This dreadful, inconceivable punishment, invented by the imagination of delirium, caused the novice to start, and a harsh short laugh issued from his throat—he had just seen the Inquisitor Arbues under the form of a tiger with a goose's head and feet, when an almost complete prostration of strength came over him; and when they came to seek for him to take him back to the church, he could scarcely sustain himself; he walked slowly and with tottering steps, his pale face drooped on his breast, and a painful sigh escaped from his bosom. But when he drew near the altar and perceived Pierre Arbues seated in his episcopal chair, the sight appeared to revive him, a flash of hatred darted from his dark eye, the blood flew back to his heart, and he again returned to the realities of life. Then he humbly kneeled on the bare stones, no longer accompanied by his adopted father, as he had been at the beginning of the ceremony, but alone; he had no other father but God.

He pronounced the vows in a firmer voice. The prior received them, and when they were concluded the organ recommenced its sublime harmony, and the monks thundered forth the *Te Deum.*

The music over, they stretched out the newly professed monk upon a bier, and began the prayers for the dead. While this was going on, José, overcome by emotion and fatigue, was wrapt in a deep slumber. It appeared as if the tomb was the only place of peace and repose for him, the dead clothes in which he was wrapped had separated him from life, and all the ills that follow in its train.

The movement made by the monks when they lifted up the coffin to convey it to the catacombs was not sufficient to waken the young monk, and when he awoke from his lethargic sleep he was alone in the subterranean caverns of the abbey, surrounded by tombs and dry bones.

Such were the ceremonies that accompanied the profession of a Dominican monk; but once admitted to the order he was soon initiated into all the selfish enjoyments of a monastic life, unless indeed he had taken all this mummery for a reality.

When José awoke a deep sigh escaped from his chest, and he cast a sad look around him.

"Death!" he cried, "yes, death is sweet; it reunites—but for me: I must not yet die. No!" he cried, energetically, "no! before I die I must be avenged! Fernando," he continued, in a low tone, as if he spoke to some invisible being, "Fernando, wait a while—soon!"

CHAPTER X.

AN INQUISITOR'S PASSION.

OLORES, miraculously delivered from the persecutions of Pierre Arbues, lived peaceably, for two months, under the protection of the apostle, in the asylum he had chosen for her. For the last two months also, the unfortunate Manuel Argoso, the old Governor of Seville, languished unknown in the dungeons of the Inquisition—vast sepulchres, from which it is a matter of astonishment living beings could ever again issue.

Notwithstanding the researches and zeal of Enriquez, appointed through the influence of the Inquisitor Governor of Seville, the latter had been unable to discover the retreat of Dolores Argoso, concealed in the Abbey of the Carmelite nuns, under an assumed name. His vile passion had increased, and feeling himself unable to succeed, a devouring internal rage gnawed the heart of this filthy priest, who every day endeavoured to feed his vengeance on the unhappy wretches he was called upon to sentence.

Urged onwards by the whisperings of José—the perverse instincts of his nature roused into action by the young monk, who appeared as if he were his evil genius—Pierre Arbues heaped upon his own head the curses of Spain, but neither the sight of the punishments, nor the melancholy solemnities of the scaffold, could assuage his brutal emotions at the remembrance of the fair Andalusian.

When he cast the weight of his indignation and anger on the governor, he had no other object in view than to force the unhappy girl to yield herself up to him, out of fear for her father's life, and like a skilful intriguer, he had judged the heart of women correctly. To have arrested her, to have cast her into the dungeons of the Inquisition, to have subjected her to torture, or to death—what effect would it have produced?

The heroic girl could have suffered and died, for she loved! But to attack her father, to give him up as a victim to the tormentors of the Inquisition, to devote him to ignominy and the scaffold ; was that sufficient punishment for the governor's daughter? To see her old and honoured father given up to the executioners of this redoubted tribunal, that father who had loved her with such tender affection, who had made her life so happy, that she had not even felt the want of a mother; that was a misery on which the courage of the maiden must be wrecked.

Pierre Arbues was vexed at one thing only, he had not been able to discover her; vainly did the militia of the church seek her out, vainly did the mysterious brotherhood with their wily chief, Mandamiento, receive the most magnificent promises of money and protection : a providential power appeared to have extended itself round the young girl the holy man had taken under his protection, or rather Heaven had decreed that the moment for her persecution had not yet arrived—but that moment would not be long delayed.

The disappointment of Pierre Arbues was so deep and bitter, that even his debaucheries had lost their usual zest, the orgy was dull to him. The remembrance of Dolores alone had charms for him, and he plunged with pleasure into the deepest solitude, because it was filled with her delightful image : not that his depraved mind was sensible of real love, but in accordance with that mysterious power which declares that the wickedest man shall sometimes feel the influence of a pure and beautiful being, and without being able to comprehend its divine essence or to raise himself to that state of repentance by which man is regenerated, it makes him voluntarily and joyfully the slave of the beloved being.

A prey to these feelings, the Inquisitor of Seville had endeavoured to find, in the deep green shadows of his garden, a refuge from the phantoms that pursued him—he tried to escape from himself.

But instead of calming the agitation of his blood, the balmy breath of the orange trees then in flower, immoderately excited his brain, voluptuous torrents appeared to circulate round him, accompanied by the enervating odour. The air was as warm as it is in summer in these more northern latitudes, although it was not yet the end of April, and thousands of stars sparkled in the azure sky like so many fascinating angel looks.

And yet the night was not clear ; whitish diaphanous mists passed over every object like rapidly moving shadows, you might have taken them for a dance of sprites, the impalpable and light creations of another world, visiting this earth for an instant to preside over the awakening of nature —the joyous blossoming of spring.

No distinct sound disturbed the silence of the phantasmagoria, but the rustling of leaves seemed like a mysterious harmony of stolen kisses, and, perhaps, in the midst of the vast fecundation of all nature at the moment it awakens, the invisible and powerful hand by which it is moved produces this vague and uncertain sound, this strange and harmonious murmur, which often evades the perception of the material sense of hearing, but makes itself felt by the soul during the hours of meditation.

It was not long before father Arbues, overcome with weariness, crushed by the incessant struggles of his mind, and by that vain irritation which enervates the body and soul at the same time, fell listlessly on one of the marble seats that were placed in different parts of that voluptuous oasis.   There resting his burning forehead in his hands, tears of sorrow and vexation fell from those stern eyes whose looks made a province tremble.

An extreme weakness had come over him, and thus he remained for some time, without speaking or allowing a sigh to escape from his breast, to betray the grief with which he was devoured; and overcome, like a timid child, the inquisitorial tiger slept.

Suddenly a light footstep was heard on the gravel walk, the branches of the orange trees were separated with a loud rustling noise, and the sound as of one panting for breath, broke the silence that reigned over the spot.

In the midst of his unsound sleep, Pierre Arbues heard the sound, but at that instant he was under the influence of a species of lethargy, brought on by the violence of his former feelings; he did not open his eyes, having neither the strength nor the desire to learn what it was that thus troubled him.   He was under the delusion of a dream, and the image of Dolores which, alone, during his sleep, had appeared to his imagination; the image of Dolores, combined itself with the sound that was really heard, and the dream of the Inquisitor assumed so much of reality, that he imagined he saw the woman who was the object of his desires.

Some one in reality was approaching, and the Inquisitor thought he saw Dolores advance towards him, he stretched out his arms, and clasped the form of his favourite José, who uttered a piercing cry when he found himself thus attacked.

VIII.

Pierre Arbues opened his eyes, and perceiving the melancholy features before him, repelled José with violence, and the novice fell on the grass a few paces off; he was pale as a spectre, and his heart scarcely beat.

"Curses on the dream," exclaimed the Inquisitor; "I thought it was a woman."

José made no answer, he had not the power to speak, but his first terror soon vanished, and the Inquisitor, passing his hand over his brow like a man who is endeavouring to collect his ideas, looked at his favourite, who remained motionless and terrified, and burst into a loud fit of laughter.

"Come," he said at length, "get up, and take a turn with me through these thickets; assist me in driving away the blue devils, with which the air is filled to-night. The genii of the Giralda have been busy with me. I am dreaming, and see nothing of real life—come, José, let me beg of you to assist me to return into the world."

José, during this sally, had time to recover himself; he arose, and, saluting his eminence, inquired after his health.

"I am well, very well, my little José," said the Inquisitor, merrily.

The dreams of the night had left no trace behind them; thus it was with Pierre Arbues, he passed rapidly from one feeling to another; and this is always the case with those whose passions have much violence, and little depth. Nevertheless, the image of Dolores was not so far effaced but that it soon returned, and beset the imagination of the Inquisitor, who, as he continued to walk in the garden by the side of his favourite, gave such a turn to the conversation as was natural in the present state of his thoughts.

"José," he asked, "do you also know nothing?"

"Nothing, my lord; I have been able to discover nothing."

Both the question and answer were rather obscure; but these two men understood each other by a single word. José knew every recess in the Inquisitor's soul.

"What can I do?" murmured Arbues, angrily; "I have set all the militia of the church to work, I have roused with a little gold the miserable gitanos who make a trade of plots and murder!—nothing! I have searched through all the convents in Seville, nothing! Can Dolores have left the kingdom? Can that affectionate and pious girl have abandoned her father to my vengeance, to save her own head?"

Pierre Arbues was right when he said he had searched all the convents in Seville. That of the Carmelite nuns had not been excepted; but a simple circumstance saved Dolores. As she had shown no disposition to take the veil, and was strongly recommended by the apostle, she was allowed almost perfect liberty; and in the devotions of the house, she merely acted as a woman of the world, and a good Catholic. Dolores had a great fondness for flowers, and she had chosen a solitary spot in the immense garden of the abbey, where she cultivated with her own hands such plants as she loved the most, and when the Inquisitor paid his visit she was at a considerable distance from the building.

Pierre Arbues had also asked the abbess whether she had any novices or newly-professed nuns, besides those he was acquainted with, but

Dolores being neither one nor the other, and the abbess looking upon her as a boarder whose stay would be but short, had said nothing about her being in the convent to the Inquisitor. Thus it arose neither from prudence nor precaution, but forgetfulness; and this is the reason the Inquisitor was persuaded that the governor's daughter had left Seville.

"My lord," said José, "if this young girl has really attempted to escape from the Inquisition, cannot you write to the tribunals of Arragon and Castille, to those of Malaga and Cuenca, and to all others in Spain, nay, even to the king himself, that the sbirri of the Holy Office may be every where set on the track of the fugitive?"

"No, no!" answered Arbues sharply. "It is not her death I wish for, it is herself, herself alone."

"Is not the governor of Seville in the prisons of the Inquisition?"

"Certainly, and that is why I cannot understand why she should have fled, she is so strong-minded and courageous, and she loves her old father so much. Oh! would that she would come, would that she would come!" he continued in a species of delirium, "with what pleasure would I say to her, 'Your father is free, if you will be mine;' and she would give herself up to save her father!"

"And her father would not be saved," murmured José, at the same time looking at the Inquisitor like a hyæna.

"What's that you are muttering, José?" said Pierre Arbues.

"I was thinking what new torments might be invented to frighten the girl in case she is found."

"Who goes there?" cried Arbues, suddenly, at the same time drawing back.

"Your faithful Enriquez, who has been seeking you, my lord," said the new comer. It was no other than the governor of Seville, formerly a familiar in the Holy Office.

"Why do you intrude in this manner?" said Arbues in a very ill humour.

"I bring good news to your eminence," answered the governor, humbly, "and I thought—"

"Well, go on, what is it?"

"Dolores Argoso—"

"Well!"

"Is in the convent of the Carmelite nuns, on the opposite bank of the Guadalquivir."

"Dolores! Since when!"

"These two months."

"Thou liest," cried the Inquisitor, "I visited the convent myself, and Dolores was not there."

"She is there, my lord, I swear to you, by Heaven; I am certain of it, and I will prove it to you."

"My brave Enriquez," cried the Inquisitor, with a burst of joy, "my brave Enriquez! how have you discovered this?"

"My lord," answered the familiar, making an awkward bow, "I trust your eminence will grant me absolution for my sin. I disguised myself as a monk, and confessed the abbess."

"By G——d,' cried Pierre Arbues, "such an idea never entered my head; priest, although I am."

"Does your eminence grant me absolution?" said Enriquez, with a downcast look.

The Inquisitor made the sign of the cross in the air, and the new Governor of Seville proudly raised his head, and stood like a man who understood the value of his services.

"'Tis well," cried the Inquisitor, rubbing his hands, "and now for you and I, my proud Lucretia. Let us go in," he continued, "and Enriquez will give me an account of his government. How does heresy get on?" continued Pierre Arbues, as they moved on.

"My lord, it is drawing nearer and nearer, and the convents themselves are not exempt from the leprosy."

"The deuce!" cried the Inquisitor, "we must take good care to freshen our Catholic zeal, by treating all those as heretics who do not denounce heresy. How many have been arrested this week?"

"Only about fifteen or twenty persons, my lord."

"People of consideration?"

"Yes, for the most part; two or three doctors in divinity, who have thought fit to find fault with the latin text of the vulgate, and several others of the same stamp, who, while they call themselves Catholics, are zealous admirers of Martin Luther."

"Among these," said Arbues, "are some I peculiarly hate—John d'Avila, Luis de Grenade, and others, who are styled apostles, and employ all their eloquence against the Inquisition; but let them beware, they will be shivered like glass if they attack it."

"My lord," said José, "have you not the power of silencing them?"

"Yes," exclaimed Pierre Arbues. "I am weary of their preaching, which has, at least, the effect of inspiring men with a wish for liberty; they make themselves simple and humble, that they may be powerful; but, by Heaven! every word they utter is like the blow of an axe in St. Peter's chair; and if Heaven's Vicar understood the true interests of the church, he would give me full license to act against them, to burn them like simple laymen, for they are heretics notwithstanding their ecclesiastical character, and they have separated themselves from the Roman Church in their hearts."

"My lord," said José, "to destroy the tree you must tear up the roots; as long as a single heretic remains in Spain, heresy will be reproduced like those ill weeds, of which you dare not leave in the earth the fragment of a root."

"We will take good care of it," replied the Inquisitor; "and by the Virgin, we will dig up the very earth from beneath their feet, that we may destroy them."

Speaking thus, they arrived at the door of the Inquisitor's apartment.

"Come, José," said Pierre Arbues.

"You must excuse me, my lord, I have to compose a sermon for to-morrow."

"And after the sermon, you will accompany us to the Carmelite convent?

"I am at the orders of your eminence," replied the favourite, and he left the room, leaving Arbues and the new Governor of Seville alone.

José had scarcely left the Inquisitorial Palace, when a woman, clothed entirely in black, addressed him; seeing by his Dominican habit that he belonged to the Holy Office, she advanced towards him with clasped hands, and with an accent of the deepest sorrow, said—

"Reverend sir, enable me to see lord Arbues."

"Who are you?" asked José, in surprise. "What business have you with the Inquisitor?"

"I want to beg my father's life," replied the young girl, in an excited state, "my father who is innocent, although accused of heresy; my father who was Governor of Seville, and now——

"Dolores!" exclaimed José, looking with curiosity at the noble features of the young girl, half hidden by the black lace of her mantilla.

"How do you know my name?" she cried, trembling.

"Dolores Argoso," continued the Dominican, in a voice at once gentle and tender; "Dolores Argoso, avoid this house, where dishonour or death await you."

"How do you know that?" she asked, in terrified accents.

The Dominican drew Dolores after him, and she allowed herself to be led away without resistance.

"Come, poor child," continued the young monk, hurrying Dolores from the inquisitorial palace; "come, if you would remain innocent, if you would wish to save your father, conceal yourself, oh conceal yourself from Pierre Arbues!"

"Well, then," she said with renewed confidence, for, in spite of his terrible livery, the Dominican had an irresistible tone of affectionate melancholy in his voice; "well, then, what must I do to save my father?"

"Conceal thyself, and let me act; confide thy cause to me, maiden."

"To you?" she answered, looking wildly at him, for she that instant recollected he belonged to the Inquisition.

"Yes, to me," he said bitterly, "to me, for under this sinister habit I carry a warm heart."

"He is so young!" thought Dolores, as she contemplated the noble features and delicate white hands of José by the pale light of the night. "Oh God! why are you a Dominican?"

"To save you, perhaps," said José, tenderly; "believe me, young maiden, and seek not to penetrate the mystery of my life; the dress sometimes is merely a mask to conceal a wounded heart."

"And you also—" cried Dolores, who felt herself attracted to the young monk by some irresistible sympathy.

"Think not of me, think of yourself alone; what is it you now propose to do?"

"As God wills it."

"Where will you conceal yourself?"

"I will return to the Carmelite convent."

"Be careful not to do that," said José; "the Inquisitor has discovered your retreat, and to-morrow he intends to satisfy himself of the truth of a report which has been made to him on the subject."

" How can he have learnt that ?" asked Dolores ; " the apostle told my name to no one, not even to the abbess."

" Poor child, you ask how the Inquisition violates the secrecy and the conscience of every one. It knows every thing. I tell you nothing is inviolable for it, not even the tomb."

" Oh my God! my God!" said Dolores, as she buried her face in her hands, and gave free vent to the tears that choked her.

" Calm thyself, calm thyself, sister," said José, using that gentle term to inspire the young girl with greater confidence, and also because a community of suffering attracted him to her.

" It is true, father, we are not even allowed to weep."

" No," said José, " the sounds of grief irritate the tiger, and his thirst for blood becomes more ardent."

" Speak lower, lower, father, they may hear us."

" Yes, you are right ; there is a babbling echo in every stone—silence, silence, then : but before you leave me, say what is to become of thee."

" Be satisfied," she said, " I have an asylum, and you promise to save my father."

" By the soul of the being I most loved, if thy father dies," said José, " it will be because I shall be unable to help him, and that you could not save him, even if you sacrificed yourself entirely for him ! Do you hear me, Dolores ?"

" I believe you," she said, clasping his hands, which she covered with tears, " I believe you ; but where can I see you again, father ?"

" Listen," said José. " At the extremity of the street of the Bohemians, in the faubourg of the Triana, there is a horrible, filthy place, called the tavern of Buena Ventura, a perfect nest of vultures, where theft, murder, and brigandage, meet each other every evening ; the aspect of the place is repulsive and dismal, there you will hear nothing but derisive laughter or frightful curses. The place is frequented by all that is most impure in Spain—bandits, women of pleasure, Bohemians, and monks. And there words as blasphemous as they are obscene, issue from the mouths of monks ; drunkenness confounds in one common brutal state those whom society rejects, and those who arrogate to themselves the right of directing it. There the most shameful crimes are contrived—assassination, unjust persecutions, and false informations, a two-edged poniard whose wound is certain death, nocturnal abductions, murders, and violation ; for in this disgusting hot-bed instruments are found for every crime."

" What is it you mean, father ?" said Dolores.

" There," continued the monk, " there you must seek me."

" Do I dream ?" cried the poor girl. " What is it you ask me to do, father ?"

" You went to the Inquisitor's house this evening ; well, believe me, maiden, the place of which I have drawn so horrible a picture is a thousand times less dangerous to you than the palace of Pierre Arbues."

José's eyes sparkled with sombre fire, and his cheeks, usually so pale, became burning red, he appeared as if consumed with an internal fever.

Dolores imagined he was mad.   But suddenly softening his voice, José looked tenderly at Dolores, and said——

"Poor child, fear not to go where José tells you ; I would save your life at the price of my own.   The tavern of Buena Ventura," he continued, "belongs to an alguazil named Coco, a good and honest lad, devoted to my service, and to his sister, La Chapa, an excellent girl, who would cast herself into the Guadalquivir to do good to any one. These good people are poor, and they earn their living the best way they can.   But you may rely upon them ; if you want my assistance you have only to say to Coco and his sister, ' I want to see Father José,' and you will see me again ; but be cautious—go out at night only, and then in disguise."

"Fear not, I will not compromise you ; but," she continued, " have I nothing to fear ?"

"Nothing," said José ; "no one will ever suspect you frequent a place like that, only come dressed like one of the common people."

Thus speaking, they arrived at the Triana-bridge.   When they had crossed it, José turned to Dolores, and said——

"Which is your road now ?"

"This way," she said, pointing to the river bank on her right.

"And I," said José, "go this way.   Adieu, Dolores, rely on me ; but remember, you must only mention my name in the presence of two persons, the alguazil Coco, or his sister.   Adieu, be prudent."

José went up the Calle de los Gitanos, and Dolores followed the river bank : the road led her to the apostle's house.

CHAPTER XII.

THE CLOTHES MARKET.

A PREY to that hallucination of mind to which all those are subject whose lives have been suddenly overtaken by calamity, Dolores in a short space of time walked the distance that separated her from the apostle's house. Notwithstanding the strange kindness with which she had been treated by a member of the Inquisition, she was not entirely free from alarm, and she longed to be once more under the protection of her holy friend.

Her desire to see the apostle again was the greater from the fact of her having seen him but once while she remained at the Carmelite convent, and that was the only time she received news of Estevan, and thus ignorant of the fate of him she loved, Dolores was filled with anxiety. "Is he still at liberty?" she asked herself in terror; and this frightful uncertainty made her heart beat quick and her footsteps become more hurried.

When she drew near to the apostle's house she was surprised at not seeing through the narrow windows the pale glimmer of the lamp that lighted the vigils of the good man, but the garden gate was unfastened; it was a kind of trellis-work formed of the light branches of the palm-tree, fixed in a frame-work of wood. Dolores knocked at the door of the house, but it was fast, and no one answered.

"Alas! he is not here," said the poor girl, alarmed at this new misfortune.

Again she knocked, loudly and perseveringly, but in vain—no one came to open it. Then Dolores ran through all the garden: it was a tolerably large enclosure, filled with fruit trees, and crowned with climbing vines; the patrimony of children and weary travellers, who stripped

.the trees of their fruit and the vines of their golden bunches with perfect freedom from restraint. The apostle allowed it; had he not, the veneration with which he inspired them would have preserved them untouched, and the slight osier barrier would never have been passed. Dolores in vain explored every corner of the rural spot. No one! It was evident that the apostle was absent; but as his solitary dwelling was far away from any other habitation, no one could inform her of his whereabouts. What should she do? She could not return to the Carmelite convent, the danger was too great. To the town? Which of her friends would she have dared to expose to the vengeance of the Inquisition, by asking an asylum? And then again every gate would be

closed against the daughter of a man accused of heresy. She had no other resource but the tavern; but the description José had given her of it made her afraid to seek a refuge there—she had rather pass the night in the garden.

The air was cool, notwithstanding the fine spring weather; but the proximity of the river made it damp. Dolores at the same time had no other covering than a robe of black silk and a lace mantilla. The trees were covered with leaves and flowers, and thick grass grew under foot. She seated herself at the foot of a large banana-tree, and allowed her long hair to fall over her shoulders like a mantle, rolled her mantilla round her head, and casting a supplicatory look to Heaven, she crouched on the earth amid the fresh thick grass. How she longed for the apostle's return!

IX.

But hours passed away, and, kept awake by her anxiety, Dolores felt the coolness of the night air.   At times footsteps were heard on the road, and then she raised her head to look around her, hoping they announced the arrival of him she expected ; but the passenger passed on, and again she fell into a state of despondency.   Close by, the Guadalquivir rolled onwards its peaceable waves with a steady monotonous sound, the cricket uttered its sharp cry in the silence of the night, and now and then the spring breeze, blowing in short gusts, swept the summits of the trees, whence a rosy and odoriferous shower would fall.   But in the eyes of the unfortunate young girl this magnificent night was full of vague terrors and sinister forebodings.

Towards the morning, overpowered by grief and weariness, she slept, but she felt chilly in her sleep.   Suddenly it seemed as if a gentle heat warmed her stiffened limbs—she was in a fairy palace.   Beneath an azure canopy that formed the immense dome of this splendid palace, a great light, as of gold, lighted by the hands of genii, gently rose towards the cupola, carried upwards by invisible beings ; and as it rose it became brighter and hotter, until at length it spread torrents of light and heat through all the palace.   But scarcely had it reached the cupola, when the magnificent palace, peopled with airy beings of marvellous beauty, suddenly changed its appearance.   The glittering furniture, the flowers that decorated it, disappeared ; the wings of the sylphides and genii fell into golden dust ; their beautiful forms became distorted, red, and transparent ; and a burning heat threatened to inflame the palace.   Dolores would have fled from the terrible punishment of the flames, but these monsters formed a circle round her to prevent her leaving, and one among them held over her head a burning mirror, beneath which she felt herself scorching, as if at the stake.

Awoke by the sufferings of her dream, Dolores opened her eyes ; the scorching sun had slowly arisen in the heaven, and poured down its rays on the features of the young girl.   She had slept long, and it was then ten o'clock.   Filled with astonishment, she looked round her to collect her ideas, which had been interrupted by sleep, and the events of the evening returning to her recollection, she was overcome with bitter discouragement.

Dolores was strong in heart and mind, but she was too young : she knew too little of the world to bear up spontaneously against sudden misfortune ; she was only really strong when danger was present.   For the common sorrows of life she had, in the first instance, tears alone ; her energy only came to her assistance after reflection : for the mind of Dolores was just and elevated, and she strengthened herself by reason. And this is always the case with women of a superior nature : their courage is but a constant struggle between their reason and their heart, excepting where the heart itself is interested, then, alone, it rivals the fiercest courage of man.   With this exception a woman's strength is merely the power of suffering calmly.   Would they be women if they were otherwise ?

Dolores remained for a few minutes overcome by this new misfortune. She looked towards the house—everything was in the same state as on the previous evening ; the windows were closed, and all was as silent as death. To be better satisfied of the fact, Dolores arranged her dress, fastened up her magnificent tresses, drew her mantilla over her forehead, and again knocked at the apostle's door; but it was in vain—he had not returned.

Dolores was alone—abandoned, without an asylum, without bread; and she dared not venture out, during the day, in the streets of Seville, fearing she should be known and stopped. She had, nevertheless, made up her mind to go to the tavern: it was her last resource, and she placed herself in the hands of Providence. But that she might not be surprised by the sbirri of the Inquisition, she resolved to wait until the evening before she entered the town.

In several parts of the garden of the apostle, lofty sugar-canes were planted; American trees, that grew so vigorously and beautiful beneath the ardent sun of Andalusia, mingled their sombre verdure with the branches of the vine, scarcely covered with its budding leaves, or the blossoming peach-trees that expanded to the sun their rose-coloured and perfumed aigrettes. Dolores selected a place of shelter in a square plantation of sugar-canes, determined there to pass the long day. She waited until evening, a prey to anxiety, and overcome with fatigue and hunger, for she had not broken her fast since the previous evening. She chewed several pieces of the sugar-cane, and drank the limpid water of the Guadalquivir to quench her parching thirst; but it was not enough to restore her strength. During this long and wearisome day many persons passed along the road, and several children entered the garden in pursuit of butterflies; these were the only incidents that disturbed the poor abandoned girl, who remained closely hidden among the branches; and no one would have imagined that the brilliant Dolores Argoso, the daughter of one of the richest noblemen of Spain, was there, like a mendicant, obliged to sleep on the bare ground, without food or shelter.

At length the sun descended to the horizon; it was the hour when almost every one in Spain enjoyed his siesta, and Dolores thought she could leave her hiding-place with safety. José had advised her only to go abroad in disguise, and she had to consider how she could obtain a dress. Dolores was without money, but her silk robe was magnificent, and her mantilla of the finest lace. She made up her mind, therefore, to go to the Rastro, a place where second-hand articles were sold, bought, or exchanged—there only could she, without money, obtain a suitable disguise. She left the garden, concealed her features, and returned by the same road as she had travelled the previous evening, for the Rastro was situated in the Barrio of Triana.

At the extremity of the street of the gitanos there existed at that time an irregular square, in which a number of dark and dirty streets ended, and where the slaughter-houses of the town were situated. On one side of this square, in wooden sheds built like houses alongside of each other, the dealers in the offal of animals were found. In front of these sheds might be seen the livers of bullocks, calves, sheep, and even pigs, suspended by iron hooks, together with the hearts and kidneys of the same animals, and other provisions of the same nature. There, in immense tubs of brine, heads, feet, and intestines, confusedly mingled, were piled on each other—all these disgusting viands, despised by the rich, were intended as food for the lower orders of Seville.

Then figure to yourself a number of badly dressed women, seated on the ground in the square, and arranged in a row, each having before her a mass of rubbish that served for a stall. Oh! if you are a lover of contrasts, certainly you cannot do better than visit the Rastro of Seville, there, even at the present day, you will find articles of every description, from the rag of which lint is made, to the court dress of a duchess—from the wooden platter, out of which the Bohemians feed, to the silver Madonna before which they kneel. Sometimes this Madonna has an old hat upon her head, destined like herself to be sold.

Further on, a coral chaplet hangs from a hook still covered with grease and filth, and a magnificent service of silver gilt stands close to some vessel of earthenware. A mantilla is sometimes hung on a broomstick, and at other times a crucifix, accompanied by a pair of pistols, is suspended from the two arms of a cross. In fact, the Rastro is a place where relics of all kinds are exposed for sale, from those of a grandee of Spain, who has been too prodigal of his revenues, to those of the unhappy wretches whose earnings have been absorbed by the rapacity of the monks. It was a confused assemblage of unmatched and hetero-geneous matters. And why need you be astonished at this strange medley of riches and misery? The dealers of the Rastro are not like those of the Temple at Paris; they do not sell on their own account, but for any one; in fact, they are confidential brokers or agents.

The church confides her Virgin to their care, that they may be enabled to purchase a more expensive image; the titled dame her jewels to pay her debts; and, sadder still, the woman of pleasure disposes of her new dresses, of which she wearies in an hour, and the manola of her Sunday garments, which she is frequently obliged to dispose of to purchase bread.

A dealer of the Rastro did everything for everybody; she was able to satisfy the most difficult; she sold and exchanged, and, in her case, as in that of all dealers, the victory was to the sharpest practitioner, but it rarely belonged to any but herself: the profit, and a large profit it was, was always on her side.

At the time of which we are speaking, this description of trading was much more extensive than at the present day, on account of the great amount of property, confiscated by the Inquisitors, that came into the hands of the informers, and was brought here for sale.

When Dolores arrived at the Place of the Rastro, she drew back in disgust, overcome by the dreadful stench; but soon after, having made an effort to overcome her feelings, she continued to advance and tremblingly approached one of the dealers, who was still tolerably young, and whose physiognomy inspired her with more confidence than that of the others. But as these women imagined she wanted to make a purchase they made a circle round her, and the hubbub of words was enough to confuse even a deaf man. Every one praised her own merchandise with more or less engaging gestures, and with a clack of words enough to fascinate a conjuror.

" Senorita," exclaimed one, " will you buy this beautiful necklace of fine pearls; it belonged to the Princess Jeanne, the daughter of Queen Isabella, and it was sold at her death by one of her maids of honour to whom she had given it."

" Here," cried another, " is an enamelled chaplet ornamented with a ruby cross, the paternosters are emeralds, and it has been blessed by his holiness the Pope. Every time you tell these beads you are entitled to a hundred days of indulgence."

" Buy this of me," cried a third, and she held up streamers of Flander's lace, whose delicate net-work was covered with arabesque embroidery.

" Senora, this ring has been blessed, and will preserve you from all kinds of enchantments."

The ring in question was merely a gold ring, extremely heavy, and having the representation of a closed hand with the thumb between the middle and index finger. It was a remnant of a Moorish superstition, adopted by the Christians, and was supposed to have the power of reversing any spell.

In spite of her sorrow Dolores smiled slightly, for she had no belief in the superstitions of the day, and no faith in spells. Luckily for her, her smile was so slight that no one noticed it, had that not been the case I know not if she would not have run considerable danger.

" Well," said the first dealer Dolores had approached, " you will have none of those things then, senorita ? Stay now, buy this beautiful image of the Virgin of me, it will be lucky to you, it was given me by a holy man, him they call the apostle. He wanted money to assist some unfortunate creatures; as for himself he wants nothing, so I gave him the money in advance, without waiting for its sale.

" The apostle !" exclaimed Dolores, " do you know the apostle, my good woman ?"

" Holy Maria !" returned the dealer, " who in Seville does not know him ? Does he not console us, and give bread to our little ones ?"

" Do you know where he is now ?" said Dolores.

" No," replied the other; " he is like the good Deity, invisible; but you can always find him when you have need of him."

Deceived in the hope in which she had for an instant indulged, of hearing where her protector was, Dolores was determined to make her exchange as quickly as possible.

" I do not wish to buy your Holy Virgin," she said, timidly; " I have no means of paying for it; but I want the complete dress of a manola (a female of the poorer classes), if you will let me have one in exchange for mine."

" In exchange for yours, senorita !" said the woman, measuring Dolores with the true eye of a dealer in clothes, who can tell at a glance the value of a garment, and observe, without touching it, the slightest abrasion of the elbow, or the whitish line caused by the dust on the hem of the newest garment, even if worn but for an hour; " in exchange for your mantilla also ?" said the cunning dame, examining the lace that covered the beautiful locks of the young girl.

" Certainly," said Dolores; " but you will give me a silk one."

And the eyes of the dealer in clothes sparkled with cupidity. She handled the satin petticoat of the maiden—it was thick and fine; and having satisfied herself that the corset and sleeves were new, she proceeded to select a gown of violet-coloured serge, and a black silk mantilla. The dress was exactly of Dolores' size.

"That will do very well," she said.

"Will that suit you?" observed the dealer.

"Oh! yes; I think that will suit me very well."

"Well, then, in that case what will you give me into the bargain?"

Dolores stared, and looked at the woman with astonishment; her dress was worth ten times that which she offered her.

"Yes; how much will you give me?" said the dealer.

"I can give you nothing," said the poor girl; "I told you I have no money."

"Ah! then, that is a very different affair. Take it, poor child, take it; and you can owe me the balance. Heaven preserve me from making a pretty girl like you uncomfortable!"

"But how shall I contrive to take off my clothes?"

"Come with me," replied the dealer; "my house is not far off."

In fact, the woman possessed a kind of wooden shed near her stall, where her husband sold broken victuals. Behind the shop was a small square room, with a single mattress spread on the ground, and an old box in which she crammed her rags. It was her dwelling, and thither she conducted Dolores.

As she helped to undress her, she saw under her gown a kind of kerchief, which covered her neck; it was of magnificent Brussels point lace.

"Senora," observed the woman, "since you have no money to give me in exchange, I will be content with this neckerchief."

"Take it," said Dolores, with an air of disgust; "besides it does not agree with new clothes; but at least give me a batiste kerchief, that this coarse serge may not hurt my neck."

The dealer brought her a neckerchief—not new, indeed, but quite clean; and Dolores was content to take it for want of a better.

When she was dressed she looked at herself in a small plate of polished tin that served as a looking-glass, and was satisfied with her metamorphosis. Her heavy and clumsy garments concealed tolerably well her elegant form, and she covered herself in her mantilla, and went out.

"Let me have your custom, senora," said the woman to her.

But Dolores heard her not, and she directed her steps in haste towards the street of the gitanos.

CHAPTER XII.

A MIRACLE.

IT may be remembered, that Enriquez, appointed governor of the very noble city of Seville, through the interest of Pierre Arbues, had signalised the first days of his power by numerous arrests, and many good and learned men and many amiable women, were groaning in the prisons of the Inquisition; alarmed for those in whom he had taken an interest, the apostle induced Estevan to absent himself for a few days from Seville, and accompany him in one of his excursions through the villages of Andalusia. Wherever he went the name of the apostle acted like a talisman; women stood by the roadside in ranks, holding their children in their arms, that he might bless them, for he was the comfort and benefactor of all the poor, be their creed what it might.

"Observe," said the monk to Estevan, "how docile these people are, and how easily they might be ruled by kindness, but, instead of this, their brains are filled with superstition; and deprived of consolation and hope, they become at the same time fanatical, weak, and cruel."

"And how easily might this be altered," observed Estevan, "with so ardent and poetical a race."

"They are more than that, they are naturally intelligent and brave, loyal and affectionate; but they have been changed into cowards and hypocrites, nay, worse than that, denouncers of their fellow-men; and were it not for my priestly character, I myself should ere now have been delivered up to the power of the Inquisition, but I am a monk, and a monk can never be wrong."

"Have a care, father," said Estevan, "your dress may be no more respected than was the episcopal dignity of Calahorra and Sègovia; but oh! my father, will not the time arrive when mankind will be unwilling to believe these horrors?"

"No doubt, my son," replied the monk.

While they thus conversed they arrived at a little village built on the summit of a hill, as frequently is the case in Spain; low houses, generally painted red and green, stretched out in a tortuous line in two rows, along the hill-top, forming an irregularly built street, at the extremity of which was a small church, whose pointed steeple rose about forty feet above the buildings.

When the two travellers reached the village, all was quiet, for it was nearly night, the villagers, returned from the fields, were silently partaking of their evening meal, a few children, nearly naked, were playing about near the half-opened doors, the savory smell of the viands came from the houses, and a few shepherds were slowly climbing the mountain side, to drive home their goats. Our travellers had passed along more than half the length of the street without interruption, but as they crossed the entrance of a low building whose dilapidated exterior bespoke poverty, they stopped simultaneously, struck by the extraordinary sound of a rude chorus of voices of men, women, and children ; the house was apparently full, and some strange event appeared to have taken place. The travellers listened for a few moments, when they suddenly heard a female voice say in a compassionate tone,

" Poor Pablo, and he was so well this morning."

" Some one needs our assistance here," said the apostle, and, pushing the worm-eaten door, it yielded to his efforts, and he entered, along with Estevan. Some twenty gitanos, men, women, children, and young girls had assembled in a filthy cabin, into which daylight seldom entered, and surrounded a man dressed in his holiday garments, and seated in a chair. The man was extremely pale, and appeared to be asleep. The whole of the gitanos with the abuela, or queen, of their strange corporation, at their head, stood round the sitting man.

At the entrance of Estevan and his companion, the gitanos did not disturb themselves ; but the abuela, who had much respect for the monk, had a little three-legged stool, the only seat in the hovel, brought out for him. Estevan remained standing, and observed,

" What is the meaning of this, father ?"

" This man is dead, and they are performing the funeral ceremonies. See."

A gitano advanced towards the deceased, and placed a mandolin in his arm, and then, in a loud voice, and without any signs of shame, he accused himself of all the crimes he had committed since the death of the last of their brotherhood, and, after this singular confession, the gitano, addressing the dead man, said,

" Play, and if I have done wrong may your music make me deaf; if I have done right, move not, and I shall consider myself absolved."

As you may well imagine, the deceased did not obey the first of these injunctions, and the gitano drew back with as easy a conscience as a usurer, who has just received absolution, under the promise of making restitution.

" What barbarism !" observed Estevan, in a whisper.

" Listen, my son," said the monk, " it is not all."

In fact, every individual present made a confession, and all the assembly felt perfectly satisfied the dead man had absolved them, and imagined they were as innocent as doves. The room was by this time lighted up with torches, and the apostle, who possessed a considerable knowledge of medicine, carefully examined the deceased man.

"The limbs of this man," he observed to Estevan in a whisper, "are still supple; he merely appears extremely pale."

"That is true," said Estevan, who examined him also.

But they were not able to indulge long in these physiological observations, for a young girl began to dance a lively and lascivious fandango before the corpse; and, by degrees, all those present, also, danced one after the other, and, taking each other by the hand, they formed a circle round the body.

At first their movements were gentle and regulated, as if they wished gradually to familiarise themselves with the measure, then the dance became more rapid, and they hurried one another forward in their

round; thus, growing by degrees more animated, they went round at so rapid a rate, that you might have imagined they were a band of demons carried forward through space by some invisible power.

Suddenly the furious troop stood still and shouted loudly. They pushed the corpse from its seat, and it fell in the midst of the circle formed around it, against a young girl, who, less active than the rest, had entangled her scarf in the metal buttons of its vest. The gitanella drew back with a horrified look, and the dead man fell with his face against the earth.

x.

" Oh heavens !" cried the Abuela, " what a misfortune it is for you, poor Marica ! that the dead man fell against you."

" Ah," observed the rest, " you will meet with great misfortunes, perhaps death, unless you will pass the night near Pablo."

" I pass the night alone with a corpse !" shrieked the terrified gitanella : " I pass the night with Pablo, to see all the infernal demons dance before him, and then carry him off !"

" I would remain with you, my poor Mariquilla," said a tall young fellow who had been looking sweetly at the Bohemian girl ; " but then your watching would go for nothing."

" Oh ! I am too much frightened," said the gitanella, shedding tears ; " I would rather die, if Pablo insists on it."

While the gitanos were thus debating this serious affair, the monk sprang towards the dead man, and stooping down for the purpose of raising him up he saw that Pablo, in falling, had slightly wounded his face, and that the wound bled.

" Silence, my children," he cried out, " this man is not dead."

Their cries ceased as if by enchantment, and all the gitanos remained chained to the spot on which they stood, in stupid astonishment. They had danced fearlessly round the dead, but they were terrified at the sight of a dead man restored to life.

With the assistance of Estevan, the monk placed Pablo on the chair, and drawing out of his pocket a small bottle he always carried with him, he caused the sick man to smell at the salts, while Estevan briskly rubbed his hands to warm and restore life to them.

At the end of a few minutes the gitano opened his eyes, colour suddenly came to his cheeks, and the reaction seemed to threaten an apoplectic fit, but the sick man soon began to breathe more freely, and slowly opening his heavy eyes, he looked around him in stupid astonishment. He was saved. It had been simply a fainting fit, followed by a state of lethargy, occasioned by drunkenness.

But when the Bohemians saw the man living, whose funeral they had just been celebrating, they fell on their knees, and the youngest ran into the street, exclaiming that the monk had performed a miracle. The restored man himself, still weak and scarcely able to support himself, kissed the hands of the apostle, saying to him—

" I was dead and you restored me to life."

" Not I, it was Heaven's doing."

" Father," said Estevan, in Latin, that he might not be understood, " why do you allow them to believe that this man has been restored to life ?"

" These people, my son, are not yet ripe for the truth ; to enlighten a nation is not the work of a day."

" Must these people then remain for ever in a state of ignorance ?"

" No, my son, no ; let the water fall drop by drop, and in the end it will create a channel for itself."

After having given a little money to the gitanos, he left the building to go through the village and administer consolation to the sick, and distribute a few small coins among the poor. He preached obedience and resignation to all, and the impetuous Estevan, in spite of his philosophical doctrines, that pointed out a more active reform, could not avoid admiring the profound judgment of the monk.

"Francisca," said a young man to his wife, "our child will be strong and handsome, for the apostle looked at him, and kissed his little hand."

"We shall have a fine harvest," said another; "he paid us a visit now the ears are just beginning to fill!"

"The lightning will respect our house," observed a third; "for the priest stopped as he passed the door."

"Heaven will bless you, because you are good," said the holy man; "and you will be happy, because you do harm to no one."

"Father," exclaimed a young woman in tears, carrying twin children in her arms, "they have put my husband in the prisons of the Inquisition because he is a converted Moor, and he omitted going to mass that he might watch over me the day these children were born."

The monk looked mournfully up to Heaven.

"Take patience, daughter," he said to the poor woman; "have confidence in Heaven; I also will look after you."

"He is a real saint," observed an old woman, in a whisper; "he has no fear of the Inquisition."

"Woman," said the monk, "those who put their their trust in Heaven, need fear nothing."

Thus closed the day, and, in the midst of the benedictions of the villagers, Estevan and the monk departed, and took up their lodging in one of those verdant cabins the shepherds erect on the hills to watch over their flocks.

CHAPTER XIII.

JOSÉ AGAIN.

TO Dolores let us return, who was left directing her steps to the tavern. When she reached the extremity of the street of the gitanos, she easily recognised the sign of the "Buena Ventura," which was written in large characters on the wall, and, in spite of the increasing darkness, Dolores could not be deceived.

As yet there were few people in the tavern; two or three monks were in conversation over their jug of wine, and at one end of the table an ill-dressed man and woman were eating a piece of black bread with onions; a couple of pewter mugs, and a goblet of the commonest wine stood before them, while the small lighted candles placed against the wall threw a doubtful light over the room.

The quiet that pervaded the place somewhat reassured the governor's daughter, but she still hesitated for a few seconds, for not seeing La Chapa she did not know to whom to address herself; but Coco's sister soon made her appearance from the kitchen, and then Dolores taking heart pushed open the door and walked strait up to the young hostess; when she was close to her she drew aside her mantilla, and La Chapa at once recollected her. But Dolores also, at the same time, recognised the girl who had been the messenger in the horrible plot, of which she had been the victim, and she drew back with a look of horror. La Chapa looked at her with a supplicating air, and, with the perfect presence of mind of an Andalusian, she eagerly took her by the hand and pretended to kiss her on both cheeks.

"And is it you, my poor Anna?" she said, in a happy tone; "who would have said I should have the pleasure of seeing my good cousin to-day. Come then," she continued, leading Dolores to the little recess in which she cooked the *puchero*, "come along, and let us have a chat about my aunt and your brothers, my poor little Anna. How happy I am to see you"

While she was pouring forth this flood of words, La Chapa had withdrawn Dolores from the gaze of the people in the tavern; and the latter, who could scarcely support herself for emotion, sat down in an old rush-bottomed chair that stood in a corner.

"Take courage, senora," said Coco's sister in a whisper, and almost going on her knees; "take courage and fear nothing, I would lose my life to save you; but," she added, seeing that Dolores was resuming her confidence, "seem as if you were talking to me, as if you were my cousin; we must deceive those who are watching us."

At this instant a monk called for a jug of wine, and La Chapa, ever active and ready, hastened to serve him.

"My poor little cousin," she observed to the woman who sat at the end of the table; "how kind it is of her to come and see me."

But the woman La Chapa addressed was the only one to whom Dolores was not unknown—it was Culervina. The serena smiled, but said nothing; a few minutes afterwards she went up to the hostess, who had gone to the door to see if her brother was returning.

"Chapa," she said, "take great care of your cousin, and if she stands in need of me or Manofina, you know where to find us. I know your cousin," said the young Bohemian, in a whisper.

"Then be cautious, and say nothing," said La Chapa.

"What are you afraid of? She is a protégé of the apostle, and I love her as much as you do; only remember what I said to you, if she needs our assistance come and seek us. Adieu."

"Let us have a look at your cousin, Chapa," said a big-bellied monk, who was beginning to be affected by the fumes of the wine. "Is she as pretty as you are, my little one?"

"Oh the poor child, let her be quiet," replied La Chapa; "she is as timid as a lamb."

"But that does not prevent her being pretty."

"You shall see her after she has had a nap," said La Chapa; "she has walked several leagues, and is dreadfully fatigued."

The entrance of a number of working men, who came in to sup, put an end to this colloquy, and the monk went on drinking. La Chapa, after she had served all her customers with remarkable quickness and skill, took advantage of the attention they were paying to their meals, and the noise their hungry jaws made as they ate, to converse in a whisper with the governor's daughter.

"Chapa," said Dolores, who had somewhat overcome her distrust, "do you know José, the monk?"

"Know him!" she exclaimed; "he is a saint, senora—although," she added in a whisper, "he wears the dress of the Inquisition. He came yesterday, and told me if you asked for him he was to be sent for."

"Ah!" said Dolores, breathing more freely, "he did not deceive me, then."

"As for me," said La Chapa, almost in tears, "have you forgiven me?"

"Yes," replied Dolores, "I pardon you, although you have done me much harm."

"Alas, I knew not what I did, I obeyed my directions, that was all; oh, if you but knew what one is obliged to do to save one's life!"

The governor's daughter was extremely pale, for she had eaten nothing the whole day; but having told her wants to La Chapa, the latter served her with a cup of chocolate, of which she partook. She had scarcely made an end of her slight repast when an unusual sound was heard in the eating-room, and she advanced her head a little.

Everybody had risen spontaneously, with a feeling of respect and deference: the Inquisitor's favourite had just entered the room. Even the sons of St. Francis themselves were not afraid to give the young Dominican this public testimony of submission and respect.

José himself moved proudly through the midst of the bowing assembly. He went directly to the kitchen, and Dolores turned towards him her beautiful face that bore the marks of sorrow and distress.

"Here, already?" said José, as he recognised her.

"Already?" she replied meekly; "that phrase, father, seems like a reproach: do you, also, already repent the protection you have granted me?"

"Certainly not, poor child," said the young monk; "what I have promised I will perform with pleasure; but be not astonished at my surprise. Did you not tell me, yesterday, you had an asylum?"

"I thought so, father; but the party I sought was gone, dead perhaps. I passed the night among the rushes, and this evening I procured with great difficulty this humble dress to disguise myself."

"You acted prudently, for you are more in danger than ever; but I have provided against it, and no one," he added, smiling bitterly, "no one will suspect the Dominican José of procuring an asylum for a woman pursued by the Inquisition."

"Father," said Dolores, with some uneasiness, "where then will you conduct me?"

"Do you doubt me, Dolores?" asked José, fixing his frank and ardent eye upon her.

"Oh, pardon me; but every step I take leads me to the brink of an abyss and yet— Oh! I believe you, I believe you! if you wished to betray me you would not look in that manner. Do what you will with me," said the governor's daughter, almost throwing herself on her knees before this extraordinary man.

Two bitter scorching tears glided slowly from the long eyelashes of José, down his pale and somewhat attenuated cheeks.

"You weep, father," said the young girl, tenderly, "alas! you also ought not to have been born in this iron age."

"Heaven," replied José, "places us here, when and for what purpose it pleases, and sometimes it makes the sufferer the instrument of its eternal vengeance. This perhaps, Dolores, is the reason you and I live in such an age."

"Your melancholy terrifies me, and yet I rely upon you, and will go wherever you wish to conduct me—and then," she added, with a little hesitation, "I had still something to ask of you."

"Speak," said José, who almost guessed at her meaning.

"I was affianced to Don Estevan de Vargas."

"I know it," said José, suppressing a melancholy sigh, "make your heart easy; Don Estevan is safe."

"You have saved him, then?" she exclaimed, joyfully.

"No, I have not saved him, but Eternal Justice has. I am but the obedient agent."

In the meantime, Coco had returned, and José took him on one side.

"Coco," he said, "while your sister is engaged, follow me and this young girl to the gates of the town."

"Let it be as your beatitude desires," answered Coco, inclining his head; "but do you mean, both of you, to pass through the crowded room?"

"You and I will pass through it alone; the young girl will go out by the little door at the back of the house."

The Dominican left the tavern in the midst of the respectful salutations of the noble assembly, and Coco joined him in the street, a few minutes afterwards; they both together went round the house, and re-entered it from the lane in the rear. Dolores was ready to leave. She bade La Chapa adieu, and followed José, who acted as guide, for even the alguazil was ignorant of the place to which they were to be led.

"You are not alarmed, anyhow?" said José, pressing the trembling hand of Dolores Argoso.

"See," she said, resting on his arm with noble confidence.

They all three left the tavern unnoticed by any one.

CHAPTER XIV.

THE ABBESS OF THE CARMELITES.

N incident of another description occurred at the abbey of the Carmelites, while this scene, rather uninteresting it is true, but necessary to the development of our tale, was taking place at the tavern of the Buena Ventura.

The abbess, the descendant of a princely house, was enthroned, surrounded by a few of her favourites—yes, enthroned, for this humble daughter of St. Francis was seated in a large velvet arm chair, raised on a stage with several steps, and surmounted by a canopy ornamented with golden fringe.

Near to her was the crosier or pastoral staff, an emblem of her dignity. A long rosary of emeralds and filigree work, depended from her waist: finally, a large cross of chased gold sparkled on her breast, and every movement of her white and delicate hand caused her abbatical ring, in which a single diamond of the first water was set, to glitter enough to dazzle the eyes.

The abbess was about four and twenty years of age. She was a woman of the middle height, but appeared taller, so proudly she bore her shoulders, and so firmly and erect was her beautiful head detached from the sweetest neck in the world. Her colour, whiter than is usual among the Andalusian women, had become still fairer from the shelter of the cloister, and her dark blue eyes shone with metallic lustre from beneath her jet black eyelashes. Still the features of the abbess had no other distinctive character beyond the pride of birth, and a strong impress of sensuality, a feeling plainly marked by her rosy and voluptuous lips, shaded with a light down almost as dark as that of her eyebrows, and soft in the extreme.

But the dominant passion of the abbess was pride, and she delighted in those who best knew how to flatter her aristocratical vanity; she wished to be a queen, even in the cloister.

Around her were seated her favourites, on less elevated seats, talking, or busy at needlework.

At this moment a great event occupied the attention of the holy maidens—the disappearance of Dolores.

" Clara," said the abbess to a young nun, seated near her, " can you understand the reason this young girl left the convent, when I treated her as a sister ?"

"No, really, mother, I cannot," replied the Carmelite nun, "at least unless she was shut up here to wean her from some worldly affection, to which she has returned."

"She was the model of modesty," said the abbess, "and notwithstanding her somewhat proud and reserved manner, her disposition was admirable; I really thought I should have been able to have attached her to our humble flock."

"What a pity she should have gone to lose herself in the world," said a novice, whose sparkling eye was far from expressing the perfect quietude of her feelings and mind; "where will she be more happy than she would have been amongst us?"

"Daughter," replied Frances de Lerma, "thank God, who, in snatching you from the same danger, allows you to pass your life here in peace."

The young recluse suppressed a sigh as she forced her features into an expression of content.

"You must acknowledge, mother," she continued, spreading out upon her knees a large band of white watered silk, embroidered with gold flowers of exquisite delicacy, "you must acknowledge that this is a beautiful altar-cloth, and that no convent in Seville can boast of one like it."

"It is really admirable," replied the abbess, "and it will be a worthy ornament to our chapel on the day you take the veil, my daughter. But what have you there, Catherine?" she continued, addressing a very young nun who was turning over, beneath her veil, a badly printed book, ornamented with cuts even more rudely executed than the text itself. The nun slightly blushed, and hid the book in her pocket.

"Let me see it," said the abbess, sharply.

Catherine had been rather spoiled by the abbess; on account of her amiable disposition, and more particularly owing to the large fortune and elevated rank of her family; Catherine held out the book with a discontented look, and her companions were enabled to read on the cover these words, printed in large letters, "*The Holy Bible!*" It was a Protestant Bible translated into Spanish and printed in Holland.

"It is a book of devotion," observed Clara, "it was well worth your while making such a mystery of it."

"Yes, but it is a Lutheran Bible," said the abbess, less ignorant, but quite as curious as the rest; "where did you get that, Catherine?"

"From my mother's brother, madame; he brought it from Flanders when he was in command of a regiment. My uncle was a great partisan of the reformed religion, and when he gave me the book he said, 'Niece, you will not be shut up for ever; when the reform of the great Luther shall have penetrated into Spain, the nuns will be free, and they will be able to marry, as they do in Germany.'"

"Oh mother, what sacrilege!" cried the recluses, who listened with incredible eagerness.

"Silence, Catherine," said Frances de Lerma; "it is imprudent to say so, my daughter."

"Is it far from here to Germany?" observed the ignorant Clara.

"Oh, certainly," replied Catherine, "but we shall be all dead when Luther comes."

"Silence! silence!" cried the impetuous abbess, whose heart beat violently at the mere idea of liberty. "Oh!" she thought to herself, "liberty for us also?—but we shall be dead before it arrives," she murmured, repeating Catherine's words.

"Our mother is thoughtful," said Clara, in a whisper.

A loud ring at the bell startled the recluses.

"Clara," said the abbess, suddenly recollecting herself, "see who that is—I do not expect a visitor at this hour."

Before Clara could reach the door, a lay sister entered with a letter. The abbess broke the seal, and after reading the first few lines, she stood up.

"Sisters," she said, "let us go and meet the Grand Inquisitor, Pierre Arbues, who does us the honour of visiting us;" and the abbess placed herself at the head of her nuns, and proceeded to the convent-door to meet the Inquisitor.

When they arrived at the gate of the cloisters, Arbues descended from his litter. He advanced towards the nuns, and as soon as he had

XI.

crossed the threshold, the abbess knelt before him to receive his blessing ; the nuns did the same ; two arm chairs covered with gold fringe were brought out, in which the abbess and the Inquisitor seated themselves.

Pierre Arbues' looks were dark and lowering, and he eyed with displeasure the female assembly.

" Sister," at length, he said, " I wish to speak with you alone ; let our sisters retire."

The abbess made a sign, and they disappeared like a flight of birds. The Inquisitor, having himself seen that the doors were fast, returned to the abbess and seated himself.

" Madame," he said, " the last time I paid a visit to this community, I asked you if you had not a nun or a novice among you whom I had never seen.   You told me no, I believe."

" And it was true, my lord, there was no nun who was unknown to your eminence."

" No ; but there was a woman here you concealed from me."

" I did not conceal her from you," replied Frances de Lerma ; " she was not here when you did me the honour of visiting us ; and, besides, as she was neither a nun nor a novice, I did not think it necessary to mention her to your eminence."

" It was the very woman I was in search of."

" No doubt of it, my lord," said the abbess, in a tone of irony.

" A truce to your sarcasms," replied the Inquisitor, rudely.   " The woman I wish to see is here."

" You should have mentioned it sooner, my lord ; this woman, or rather this young girl, has left without my knowing why she has left, for I showed her every kindness."

" Gone !" exclaimed the Inquisitor, " gone !   Oh ! you deceive me, madame.   Dolores Argoso is here, and you must let me see her directly."

" Dolores Argoso ?   That was not the name of the young girl who was with me, my lord ; she was called simply Maria.   She was an orphan, placed under my care by that holy man John d'Avila."

" John d'Avila !" replied the Inquisitor, in a harsh voice, " he belongs to the barefoot Franciscans ; all these mendicants of St. Francis are our enemies."

" What has John d'Avila done to you, my lord ?" said Frances, who, with a woman's love of mischief, felt a pleasure in irritating the temper of the Inquisitor.

" What has he done, madame ?   All these preaching monks are detrimental to Rome ; they cause the Holy Inquisition to appear to the people a tyrannical power, and its zeal a species of cruelty.   But this woman, this girl," replied the angry Dominican, " let her be produced, madame ;   I tell you she is here, and I must see her."

" My lord," replied the abbess, " I told your eminence that this young girl had disappeared ; your eminence will do me the honour of believing my word."

" Frances !" cried the Inquisitor, looking angrily at the abbess.

" Pierre Arbues !" exclaimed Frances de Lerma, whose features were suddenly inflamed with anger and jealousy—" do you then think I ought to become the guardian of your mistresses? This girl is gone, what have I to do with it? Let your sbirri and familiars seek her."

"By Heaven, you are bold, madame, thus to play with the Inquisition; do you know what I can do, and who I am? Frances de Lerma, do you know?"

"I know you to be a wicked priest, a shameless monk who seeks the gratification of his brutal appetites at any sacrifice."

"Ho! ho! Frances de Lerma, the holy abbess of the Carmelites; what do you think Spain would say of you, if it knew of your conduct?"

"Alas! it is true," she exclaimed, with a terrified look, "it is true, I am a wretched woman, concealing vice under a holy dress, and protected by the walls of the cloister. I fearlessly give way to the devouring passion God has endued me with; but who then led my mind astray? Who seduced me into vice? When trembling and humiliated, I humbly accused myself of my depraved thoughts: who, with false and specious arguments quieted my conscience? Who lighted up in my bosom those fierce passions which in the time of my innocence arose but at intervals, and were speedily repressed? You! none but you, whose headstrong vices fed the flames of mine. You! that I had the weakness to love."

During this violent sally of the abbess of the Carmelites, the Inquisitor took notice of the Protestant Bible which Catherine had forgotten, and left in the chair. He glanced at the title impressed on the cover, and a sinister expression sparkled in his eyes at the discovery, and urged by an infernal afterthought he took the book and concealed it beneath his tunic; then casting his eyes on Frances, too much excited to have noticed his action, Pierre Arbues looked with admiration on the ardent and passionate woman, rendered still more beautiful by her anger; a glow of colour lighted up the pure white of her cheeks, and her eyes beamed with so lively a flame, you might have imagined they were about to dart forth sparks of fire.

The anger of the Inquisitor was appeased in an instant; never had Frances de Lerma appeared so beautiful. The serious features of Dolores, could not at that instant have borne a comparison with the incomparable beauty of the abbess of the Carmelites. In the eyes of a man like Pierre Arbues, Frances had the benefit of the comparison; and, then, Dolores was absent.

"How beautiful thou art, Frances!" exclaimed Pierre Arbues, who had gazed on her for a few moments in mute admiration. "Beautiful sinner!" he exclaimed, taking hold of the abbess's fair hand, which anger had made as cold as marble.

"Pierre!" exclaimed the nun, falling on her knees pale and exhausted, by a sudden reaction of feeling; "Pierre! I fear for my soul."

"Foolish woman!" cried the priest, and Dolores was forgotten.

CHAPTER XV.

THE CAVALCADE.

THE apostle, after having visited, in company with Estevan, the poorest villages in the neighbourhood of Seville, resolved to make it the limit of his journey, for he was uneasy respecting Dolores. The time for celebrating the auto-da-fé was at hand, and he was afraid the hour had arrived when he must endeavour, not to save the unhappy governor of Seville, that he dared not hope, but at least to console his unhappy daughter. Estevan partook of the fears of the apostle. They drew near to the Moorish town; both were on foot, like the prophets of old. It was about six o'clock in the evening, great crowds of people were moving about, for it was the hour when the numberless monasteries of Seville distributed the *melopia* (broken victuals) to the paupers and vagabonds of the city. Two young and robust lay brothers carried an enormous copper cauldron by means of a stick passed through two handles, all rushed forward with their wooden bowls to receive their rations, and discordant cries and angry shouts greeted the appearance of the savory food; but order was restored at the appearance of a third lay brother, and all were served in their turn, and by degrees the streets again became free from people.

As John d'Avila and his companion approached a group of mendicants, the former felt himself pulled by the sleeve of his garment, and, turning round, he recognised the serena.

"Will your reverence pardon me," said the young woman; "but I have been to her house, and I find no one there."

"What is the matter?" demanded Estevan, who knew she alluded to Dolores.

"Your reverence should be informed," continued Culervina, still addressing the apostle, "that the young lady you have taken under your care went a few days back to La Chapa's tavern."

"What is that? Has Dolores left the Carmelite convent?"

"I do not know," replied the serena; "but I saw her with my own eyes enter the tavern."

"Alas! what fresh misfortune has overtaken her?"

" Let us fly, father," cried Estevan.

" Imprudent man, do you not know the tavern is the rendezvous of the familiars of the Inquisition ? I will go alone ; or rather we will send forward this young woman in the first instance. Culervina go at once to Coco's house, and bring me word what has become of Senora Dolores."

" Where shall I find your reverence again ?"

" At my own house ; go my girl, and may Heaven conduct you."

The serena started off like an arrow ; and Estevan and John d'Avila hastened their steps to the house of the latter.

*   *   *   *   *

Near the Grand Place of Seville, in a bye street close to the cathedral, a small house might have been seen, whose red brick walls and architectural ornaments showed that it had been built at the same time as the Alhambra. The entrance to this building was by a low and narrow doorway, and no apparent window overlooked the street. Nevertheless, a few feet above the door a square opening had been formed, large enough to admit of the head being passed through, which was blocked up from the interior by a mass of bricks that fitted the opening to such a nicety, that when it was in its place no one would suspect the existence of any breach in the wall. At the time of our history, this building was inhabited by an elderly woman, extremely pious and attentive to her religious duties, but who received no one, with the exception of a young Dominican priest, supposed to be her confessor.

It was mid-day, and in a small room that overlooked the garden two women were conversing, while plying their needle. One of them, about fifty years of age, had a countenance expressive of the deepest sorrow—she was called Juana ; the other, in the bloom of youth, was as sorrowful as her, and as much oppressed in spirits—it was Dolores. This was the asylum in which José had placed her. Juana had been the young Dominican's nurse. Suddenly, a loud sound of trumpets was heard in the distance ; and Dolores started in her chair.

" What is the matter ?" said Juana, anxiously. " What is the matter, my child ?"

" Listen," cried Dolores, in alarm ; " listen, mother, do you not hear it ?"

The sound became louder and more animated as it drew nearer, and the trampling of horses' feet was heard.

" Oh, mother, that sound announces the triumphal march of the Inquisition. The king of executioners is passing through the streets, to let the city know that his hand has not been inactive, and that he has gathered in a harvest of victims for his approaching auto-da-fé."

The cavalcade had by this time arrived at the Grand Place, and the flourish of trumpets, louder and more distinct, fell on their ears.

" Come along, come," cried Dolores, dragging the old woman after her, and obliging her to follow her to the first story of the house ; " you shall see, mother ;" and when they reached the room that overlooked the street, from whence the greater portion of the Place might be seen, Dolores quickly removed the stone that closed the aperture in the wall.

" What are you doing ?" exclaimed her companion.

" Fear nothing, mother, no one noticed it ; they have too much to do to watch the procession of the Inquisitor,"

The Grand Inquisitor, Arbues, mounted on a white horse of the purest blood, rode on, accompanied by his retinue. The handsome features of the Inquisitor, proud, haughty, and full of energy, imposed on the people as much as his dignity. The rest of the Inquisitors followed in his train, also on horseback, and a troop of body guards escorted the cavalcade. When he reached the middle of the square, the Inquisitor stopped, and in a loud voice said—

" Brethren, in one month the very holy Inquisition will perform an act of justice on those heretics who have disgraced our holy religion. A grand auto-da-fé will take place to celebrate the victories of our great king, Charles V., in Flanders, and his zealous prosecution of heretics,"

" Oh, my God!" exclaimed Dolores, " what will become of my father ?"

The people responded to the proclamation of the Inquisitor by repeatedly crossing themselves. Again the trumpet sounded.

" Oh, my father !" again exclaimed the governor's daughter, walking about the room in wild excitement.

" Calm yourself," said Juana ; " José is coming—fear nothing."

Dolores returned to the window, and the procession had left the square, and was approaching the house.

" Oh, come away from the window," cried Juana in terror.

But Dolores paid no attention ; her eyes were fixed on the Inquisitor. The procession drew close to the house ; Dolores' face was still turned towards the street ; the room was extremely dark, and the delicate profile of the young girl indistinctly detached itself from the sides of the opening. As he passed, Pierre Arbues raised his head ; but at that instant, placing her arm round Dolores' waist, Juana succeeded in removing her from the window.

The Inquisitor started in his saddle : he again looked towards the opening where the indistinct resemblance had been seen ; but quick as lightning Juana had replaced the stone, and instead of the apparition which had startled him, Pierre Arbues saw merely a blank wall, and a house without windows. Turning towards a familiar, he asked him to whom the house belonged.

" It is the house of a poor widow on whom your almoner, Don José, bestows charity."

Juana placed the fainting Dolores in a chair. The sound of the trumpets was lost in the distance, and she remained still insensible.

Alone, and not daring to call for assistance, Juana began to feel uneasy ; when the outer door of the house opened with a slight noise, and hasty steps ascended the stairs.

" Heaven be praised," she cried ; " it must be José."

It was, in fact, José ; and the moment he entered the room Dolores opened her eyes, and sighed deeply.

" What is the matter, nurse ?" cried the Dominican.

" Father, father !" exclaimed Dolores, when she saw the young monk, " you see plainly they will kill my father !"

" Comfort yourself, Dolores ; who has told you they will kill your father ?"

" Did I not this instant hear the cries of death ? Have they not just proclaimed an approaching auto-da-fé ?"

" What does that prove ?" replied the young Dominican. " If it were intended your father should be a victim, am I not there to watch over him ?"

" Alas ! you deceive me, Don José ; your cruel pity makes you conceal the truth from me. No ! I do not believe you. Do not you also wear the livery of the Inquisition ?" she exclaimed in a state of great excitement. " Leave me ; I will throw myself at the feet of Lord Arbues ; I will clasp his knees, and I will so pray and weep, that if his soul be not as hard as a rock, he will be merciful, and give me back my father !"

" Poor maniac," said José, bitterly, looking at Juana, " do inquisitors possess a soul ? No feeling of pity ever yet moved their marble hearts ; have they ever experienced any feelings except those of pitiless ferocity, the horrid madness of unbridled debauchery, the thirst for blood, and the sight of agony ?"

" I will go ! I will go !" continued Dolores, still more excited by the dreadful picture ; and at the same time she rose, and repulsing Juana, who, taking her gently by the arm, endeavoured to soothe her. " Leave me," she cried ; " you are all in a league to deceive me : you have shut me up here as in a prison, that what is taking place should not reach my ears ; but Heaven has marred your project ; and I have learnt what you would have hidden from me. Leave me, then, leave me at liberty ; what right have you to keep me here a prisoner ?

Juana looked on her as if she thought her insane, and, relinquishing her hold of her, went and seated herself at the other extremity of the room. Dolores, finding herself at liberty, stood still, looking at José, whose pale and beautiful features were agitated by feelings of pity. The excitement of Dolores ceased at once, and, overcome by weakness, she fell into her chair.

José went up to her.

" Pardon me," she said, holding out her hand ; " I have been unjust, grief deprived me of my reason ; pardon me, Don José, but I declare to you calmly, now, that my resolution is unchangeable : I will throw myself at the feet of the Grand Inquisitor ; I am bound to endeavour to save my father's life, and it shall not be said I acted like a coward."

" You will not do so, Dolores," cried the young Dominican.

" Alas !" exclaimed Juana, " have pity on yourself."

" Fear nothing," replied Dolores ; " do you imagine I tremble at death ?"

" No ; but you dread infamy," cried José, vehemently. " Do you not then know the Inquisitor of Seville ?"

" Alas ! it is true. I thought not of that."

" Well, then, follow my advice, Dolores ; or on my soul you are lost. Let your friends act for you."

" Oh ! did I but know where Estevan was !"

" I promise you I will learn. Estevan, like myself, is solely acting for your good ; be calm and rely on us. Here you are safe ;" he added, " do not attempt to leave. My good Juana, watch over this young maiden, and see she does not leave the house."

" My noble child," said the nurse, pressing him to her breast, " may Heaven bless you for your courage."

" Fear nothing," said José, pressing her hand, " fear nothing, Juana, I will succeed in my intention."

It was night, and when he left Dolores, José directed his steps towards the Inquisitor's palace ; and to reach his place of destination, it was necessary to pass through the street in which the house of the Governor of Seville was situated. As he approached this street, José was surprised to see, at that hour, a great crowd of people filling the avenues that led to the governor's palace. The confused sound of imprecations and threats, uttered in a deep, harsh, and terrible voice, ran like a tempest blast through the angry groups ; it resembled the howling of the wind through a forest of oaks.

The crowd hastened towards the palace of the new governor ; for the people had resolved to avenge themselves. The rising had been so sudden and accompanied by so little noise, that he had not time to oppose it by means of an armed force ; a few alguazils, however, had run in from various quarters, and the dark-looking gardunos looked on without assisting either party, ready to sell their prowess to the highest bidder.

" What is the meaning of this assemblage," said José to a familiar who had been despatched thither by his eminence.

" Your reverence, it is only about an old Jewess who has just been arrested."

" Your reverence," exclaimed a courageous woman, who had overheard the familiar's answer, " the Jewess is as good a Catholic as you or I."

" What is the woman's name ?"

" She was named Maria de Bourgogne, your reverence, and is more than eighty years of age ; she was a saint who gave all her property to the poor, and that is the reason when we learnt she was in the prisons of the Holy Office, that, with one accord, we flocked to the governor's palace."

The familiar was about to cause the speaker to be seized, when José made a sign to him to retire.

" I advise you," whispered José to the courageous female, " to leave Seville as soon as possible, your late words may otherwise cost you dear."

" I believe you," she said, looking at the young Dominican, and smiling bitterly ; " and you also are an Inquisitor ?"

" I am indulgent, and I love the suffering people," said José ; " my poor woman, fear nothing from me."

The crowd became now more dense and furious, pressed forward to the governor's palace; some, armed with iron bars, endeavoured to force the bolted door, while others flourishing their formidable albacete blades in the air, prepared to defend themselves until the death; even the women, grasping their slender poniards in the right hand, rushed furiously forward. Their African blood had been awakened; hatred, the deepest, bitterest, most devouring hatred, urged them on to rebellion.

Enriquez, who had taken refuge in his palace, which he dared not leave, awaited in trembling the assistance that did not arrive; every blow that shook the door of his palace pealed in his ears like a funeral knell. The heavy mass of wood that formed the door, although studded

with iron nails, gave way before the blows applied by a thousand robust arms. But suddenly silence fell upon all, and no one dared to cross the threshold.

John d'Avila appeared at the extremity of the street.

"What is it you do?" he exclaimed; "what are you doing, madmen? Stay!"

The word ran from mouth to mouth, and at the name of the apostle, the rage of the populace was stilled like the sudden lulling of a storm. John d'Avila advanced without effort through the previously impenetrable crowd; all gave way at his approach.

XII.

"Children!" he said to them, "why do you rebel? What good will arise to you from doing so?"

"Father!" exclaimed one of the assemblage, "they have arrested Maria de Borgogne, who fed our children."

"God will restore her to you," replied the saint; "do you expect to save her by rebelling?"

At this moment, a man armed with an enormous bar of iron, stood before the monk. John d'Avila recognised Manofina.

"What is it you are doing here?" he asked, in a mild voice.

"I wish to avenge a victim," replied the bravo, without disconcerting himself; "we intend to slay that wretch, Enriquez, who has been made governor."

"You must kill no one," observed John d'Avila.

"As for that, there would not have been much harm in it—a rascal like this : but since your holiness does not wish it——"

"Heaven does not wish it, my children."

And these men, but this instant so full of violence, became at once as gentle as lambs; and as they were silently retiring, without any hostile demonstration, the sbirri approached to arrest the ringleaders.

"What would you do?" said the monk, "punish the lion for his generosity? Retire! You have no need of arms, everybody is quiet."

And the emissaries of the Inquisition submitting, in spite of themselves, to the influence of the extraordinary man, hesitated.

At this instant, José issued from the crowd; he made a sign to the alguazils, and at his mute command they retired like shadows.

In spite of his charitable feelings, John d'Avila looked with an air of distrust and dislike at the Inquisitor's favourite; nevertheless, José approached him with a confident and calm air.

"Father," he said, "she you are in search of is in safety."

John d'Avila started: he thought Dolores had been arrested by the Inquisition.

"Father," repeated José, looking meekly at him, "does not my countenance tell you I have spoken the truth?"

"Oh! restore to me the poor child Estevan and I have been lamenting."

"To-morrow, at midnight," said José, "I will wait for you at the esplanade near the fountain: meet me there, and I will conduct you to Dolores."

José disappeared; but John d'Avila said nothing to Estevan of his rencontre: he wished to go alone to the rendezvous, or perhaps he suspected some plot to entrap him.

CHAPTER XVI.

THE CONVERT.

WHEN he returned to the inquisitorial palace, Don José went before the Grand Inquisitor. Pierre Arbues was alone in his chamber, but the guards without were doubled, on account of the rioting which had taken place, and although scarcely any sound of the tumult reached his ear he was terrified to so great an extent that he expected every instant to see the door burst open by an assassin.

At the approach of José the Inquisitor raised his head.

"Well, José," said Pierre Arbues, "what news?"

"Everything is quiet, my lord; your sbirri did wonders, and the madmen were soon dispersed."

"Heaven be praised! And poor Enriquez received no injury?"

"None, my lord; they merely broke down his palace gate, and he is now as safe as your eminence."

"I am in no danger, then, José; they dare not strike so high? Perhaps I was wrong, however, in raising Enriquez to the difficult station of governor; he wants energy and resolution."

"What signifies it, my lord; he is devoted to you. The people regret Manuel Argoso; they loved him on account of his lenity, and on that account they have rebelled against Enriquez."

"Truly, these riots must be suppressed; the Inquisition of Spain must extend itself over the whole of the world, and raise itself even above the power of the Pope; the leprosy of heresy must disappear from the surface of the globe. We have about one hundred and eighteen condemned prisoners for our approaching auto-da-fé?"

"That is fifty more than the last, my lord. But," continued José, in a careless tone, "what do you mean to do with the old governor of Seville?"

"I shall treat him as he deserves, as a Lutheran heretic," cried the Inquisitor, enraged at the recollection of Dolores.

At this instant a familiar entered hastily, and handed a letter to his eminence.

"The Governor of Seville has sent this," said the messenger.

Pierre Arbues broke the seal, and read as follows :—" My lord, the abbess of the Carmelites is extremely ill, and has sent for a Franciscan to confess her. The monk is to go to the convent this evening. My letter has been written these two hours, but I have not been able to forward it on account of the riots ?"

" By Heaven !" mentally said Arbues, " she is a bold woman, to send for a wretched Franciscan, when I am her confessor.—But there is yet time.—The foolish woman may compromise me.—I must see her at once. José," he continued, " an important affair calls me away ; the abbess of the Carmelites is dying, and requires the offices of religion at my hands ; I must leave you. Adieu."

He darted out of the chamber, descended the marble staircase rapidly, mounted his litter, and started ; but when he reached the gate of the convent a Franciscan monk had just crossed the threshold, and advanced towards him. As soon as they were face to face, notwithstanding the obscurity, they recognised each other. Pierre Arbues looked sternly at the monk—it was the apostle—and he hurried through the doorway. When he reached the bedside of the abbess, Frances de Lerma, comforted by the words of the apostle, appeared to experience a moment of quiet. Unable to confide in the accomplice of her crimes, whose violence she dreaded, she sent for John d'Avila, in whose sanctity she placed implicit confidence, and by a sincere confession the unhappy woman poured out into his breast the remorse by which her soul was devoured.

" Madame," said the Inquisitor, when he found himself alone with the sick woman, " why did you send for any other confessor than myself ?"

Frances de Lerma suddenly turned round.

" Do you not know, sister, I have the power of absolving you ?"

" Before you absolve others, my lord," said the abbess, slowly, " cover your head with ashes, abase your pride in the dust, and, kneeling on the bare earth, ask for pardon for your crimes."

" The priest," replied Arbues, " however unworthy he may be, is not the less the representative of Heaven : but have you not compromised the interests of the Church in confessing yourself to a Franciscan, one of our mortal enemies ?"

" That monk, my lord, is a saint, and has comforted me, and reconciled me to Heaven ; let me die in peace, and trouble yourself no more about my soul."

Then turning round, Frances covered her head with the clothes, as if she wished to place a funeral pall between herself and the Inquisitor. And Pierre Arbues saw that her conversion was real.

The hour for the meeting of Don José with John d'Avila was near at hand. Estevan, uneasy as to the fate of her he loved, feared that the monk concealed some melancholy secret from him ; at length he ventured to say—

" Father, have you heard nothing of the poor Governor of Seville ? Has his trial yet begun, and can we do anything to save him ?"

" No," replied John d'Avila, " it has not yet begun ; until then remain concealed in your retreat. Are you ignorant of the danger of opposing the Inquisition ?"

"I will oppose it when it is necessary," replied Estevan, calmly.

"Well, then, preserve your strength for the day of battle—you will need it;" and at the same time the apostle left the house without saying a word, as he was frequently in the habit of doing: but Estevan, favoured by the darkness, after closing the door, followed John d'Avila at such a distance as not to be observed.

When he arrived near the fountain opposite the cathedral, the apostle stopped. José awaited him, seated on the margin of the fountain; but at the approach of the apostle he rose to meet him.

"Father," said José, "I would willingly have spared you this meeting, but I could not go to your dwelling without the danger of being suspected."

"Well, concerning Dolores?" said the apostle.

"Dare you follow me?"

"Why should I not dare?" asked John d'Avila. "I will follow you; lead me on, brother."

"This way, then, father," replied the young Dominican; and in a few minutes they reached the Moorish house where Juana dwelt. José then drew a key from his pocket, opened the door, and entered first; but as his companion was about to cross the threshold, Estevan advanced, and said to him, in almost a tone of supplication—

"Father, if there are dangers here, let me partake of them; and let me also see *her* once more. Is she safe?"

"At least I hope so; but I wished to have spared you what may be a deception, but since you know all, come;" and at the same time turning towards José, he said, "I do not enter without Estevan, my son."

"Estevan! let him enter, father, and see her once more."

As soon as they entered José carefully closed the door. Dolores and Juana were waiting in the lower room, and the former, who had been forewarned by José, ran to meet her deliverer; but when she perceived Estevan, whom she had not expected, she turned pale, and sank upon the seat from which she had just risen.

"Dolores," said John d'Avila, "you must bear up against joy as well as sorrow."

At his gentle voice she recovered herself, and felt ashamed that her first question had not been concerning her father.

"When does my father's trial come on, Don José?"

"The day after to-morrow," he replied; for he did not wish to deceive Dolores. "Your only hope is in producing witnesses in his favour."

Dolores for an instant made no answer; at length she addressed the apostle.

"Father, you will be a witness for him?"

"Certainly," replied the apostle; "but allow your friends full liberty of action, by not distressing them with your regrets."

While Dolores was engaged in conversation with John d'Avila, José entered the garden, as if to examine the flowers, and making a sign to Estevan, the latter followed him without hesitation.

"Don Estevan," said José, "we shall never save the governor by means of witnesses; we must seek a more efficacious plan."

"I know of no other," replied the young philosopher, too prudent to disclose his secret thoughts to a man with whom he was unacquainted.

"Don Estevan," observed José, taking the young man by the hand, "you distrust me; what have I done to deserve this injustice? I met your intended bride on the public way, overwhelmed with grief, and hastening to the Inquisitor's palace to solicit her father's pardon. I preserved her from certain death, nay, more, perhaps from infamy; I have sheltered her in my own dwelling and protected her as I would a sister; and I now am striving to save her father: what more would you have me do to obtain your confidence? Why do you mistrust me?"

"You are a Dominican."

"John d'Avila confides in me."

"And I also," said Estevan, holding out his hand.

"Well then, prove it to me, Don Estevan; if we do not succeed by witnesses, what should we do?—raise the people, carry off the governor, slay the Inquisitor?"

Estevan looked distrustfully at him.

"Such a plan would be unadvisable, unless the case were completely desperate."

The young monk pursued the conversation no further; but as he led Estevan back to his affianced, he said, emphatically, "Whatever may happen, reckon upon me, even to the death."

As they entered the room they had lately quitted, a loud knocking was heard at the door. Juana opened the door. It was Coco, who came every evening at the same hour to take José's orders, and inform him of the execution of those of the preceding evening.

"Well, what is there new, my good Coco?" said the young Dominican.

"Your reverence," replied the alguazil, with hesitation, "the late governor of Seville will, in two days, appear before the tribunal."

"I know it: what next?"

"I am placed at the door of his dungeon."

"Oh!" cried Dolores, anxiously, "can you not then—"

Coco, who divined her thoughts, observed, "I am not alone."

John d'Avila and Estevan rose to leave.

"Dolores," said the latter, in a low tone, "I will die or I will save your father."

"Bless you, Estevan," she replied.

Estevan, José, and the apostle left the room together. José accompanied them as far as the Triana bridge, and there they separated. Coco had followed the party at some distance, and José, turning back, went up to the alguazil.

"Coco," he said, "watch carefully all the movements of Don Estevan de Vargas, and whatever they may be, come and inform me without delay."

"Your reverence," replied Coco, hesitating, "it is no doubt for his good you wish me to act in this manner? A friend of the apostle."

"Be satisfied, my poor Coco; have I ever harmed any one? Speak!"

"Oh! you are as good as an angel of Heaven," replied the alguazil, "and I will do whatever your reverence requires."

CHAPTER XVII.

THE CHAMBER OF TORTURE.

N the centre of a vast rotunda, in a deep dungeon, lighted by two feeble flambeaux, four men in masks stood round another man, who, sad and feeble, could scarcely support himself; a moist and oppressive air, exhaling a fetid and sepulchral odour, spread through the vault, which was filled with instruments of torture of every description— wooden horses, iron boots, enormous nails, and cords of various dimensions, and by the side of a low wooden bench a brasier of burning coals shed its red and blue light in the dark angle of the place; numerous narrow winding stairs led to this infernal spot, and here Manuel Argoso had been led after he had been examined before the tribunal of the Inquisition, and here he awaited the arrival of the chief Inquisitor. He had allowed himself to be led, or rather carried, for he closed his eyes that he might not see the dismal passages through which he was borne; and when, with his enfeebled mind, he at length cast his eyes around upon the various instruments of torture, he thought he had left this world and arrived in that terrible place described by the evangelist.

At length Pierre Arbues arrived, accompanied by the second Inquisitor and the apostolical notary. The accused was standing in the *Chamber of Torture,* and at the sight of his judge he was recalled to the sad reality, and raising his looks to Heaven he perceived that a strong pulley had been fixed in the top of the vault, from which a thick hempen cord descended even to his feet; and he gave an involuntary shudder: the four men in masks stood around him, and strong as his courage was, he could not avoid trembling; but when he imagined that his daughter might have to submit to the same torture, all his firmness left him.

At a sign from the chief Inquisitor the torturers removed his clothing, leaving him only his shirt; then Pierre Arbues went up to him and said, with evangelical meekness, "My son, confess your crimes, and do not let your soul perish by persisting in error and heresy, and spare us the pain of obeying the just and severe laws of the Inquisition."

But Argoso answered not.

"Acknowledge all, and confess yourself." continued the Inquisitor; "we are your fathers in God, and our only wish is to save your soul;— come, a sincere acknowledgement will not only save you in another world, but it will preserve you in this, from the just vengeance of Heaven."

"I cannot acknowledge that which do not exist," replied the governor.

"I pity your impenitence, my son, and I pray to the Lord to touch your soul, which the demon has in his possession; he it is who inspires you with this culpable adherence to evil. Pray with me." And at the same time Pierre Arbues knelt by the side of his victim, and mumbled an inaudible prayer. With a holy and meek expression of countenance he made repeated signs of the cross, smote his breast, and hid his face in his hands for a few minutes. At length he rose. "Wretched child of the demon," he exclaimed, "has Heaven deigned to listen to my humble prayers and open your eyes, which are closed against the light of our holy faith?"

"My faith was always the same," replied Argoso; "it has never varied a single instant: as I received it from my father, who was a pious Christian, so shall I carry it with me to the tomb."

"Heaven is witness," observed the judge, lifting up his eyes, "it is not my fault. Proceed," he continued, turning to the torturers, "apply the question of the cord."

At these words the accused closed his eyes, a dull confused sound resounded in his ears, and a cold perspiration covered his limbs; and while every muscle trembled, the torturers drew the cord that hung from the vault towards them.

"You will continue the question, until we think proper to stop it," continued the Inquisitor, "and if during that time any injury happens to

THE QUESTION OF THE CORD.

the patient, be it the fracture of a limb, or even death itself, I protest before you all, that it is to be attributed to himself alone. And now let the will of Heaven be done," and he stretched out his hands towards the executioners.

Instantly the four masked men took hold of the unfortunate governor, and tied his hands behind his back with the end of the cord that hung above his head; then, taking hold of the other end, they raised the sufferer by the assistance of the pulley, to the top of the vault, and let him

fall down suddenly to within a foot of the ground. At this terrible shock the unhappy man nearly fainted away. The torturers waited a few minutes, until he had recovered himself, and the instant he opened his eyes they began the cruel elevation once more, and allowed him to fall again with as much violence as in the first instance. This punishment lasted for an hour.

The unfortunate governor uttered no complaint, but his panting and suffocating chest gave forth a harsh and compressed sound, resembling the death-rattle. His dim eyes became glazed like those of a dying

XIII.

man, and appeared as if about to close in the sleep of death. The cord that bound his wrists had entered so deeply into the flesh, that the blood of the tortured man streamed over his whole body, saturating the only garment he wore; and, the "question" ended. The unfortunate governor, released from his bonds, fell upon the earth like a lifeless man, his dislocated bones and mangled muscles being unable to support him.

It was a heart-rending and horrible spectacle, to see this powerful and robust man, still in the vigour of his age, overcome by this atrocious torture, and punished before he had been tried ; but what might not be expected from a tribunal which inflicted punishments like this upon the accused ! Alas ! the Inquisitors were without feeling ; they ruled by torture, and battened on agony.

"Let this man be taken back to his dungeon," said Pierre Arbues, in melancholy accents: "enough for to-day ;" and then turning to his assistant Inquisitor, he observed, "brother forget not this unhappy man in your prayers."

This was the manner in which the Inquisitors acted towards their victims ; such was their horrible hardness of heart, under the hypocritical cloak of deep piety.

Two sbirri carried out the unfortunate governor in their arms. Manuel Argoso gave no signs of life.

CHAPTER XVIII.

THE MAIDEN'S PERIL.

 T was a grand gala in Seville, the people were feasted from morning until night, the noble city celebrated the arrival of the Duke of Medina Cœli within its walls, the grand-standard bearer of the faith, who had come to assume his place in the royal auto-da-fé, intended to celebrate the numerous victories of Charles V. But while the populace were thus enjoying themselves, the noble lords and grandees of Spain were amused in the splendid saloons of the Duke de Mondejar, the son-in-law and nephew of the Duke of Medina Cœli ; and after a sumptuous banquet they had assembled in one of the magnificent saloons of his mansion. No female was admitted on this evening. It was a meeting of the "Catholic and Inquisitorial Club," of which Mondejar was president ; the meeting was in full consultation, and Pierre Arbues, who formed one of the assembly, was in earnest conversation with Don Carlos, a suitor for the hand of the daughter of Mondejar, when an attendant, raising the crimson velvet curtains that closed the entrance to the room, announced, in a loud voice, " Donna Dolores Argoso y Cevallos."

The Inquisitor started, and seeing the door of a small cabinet that adjoined the room in which they were assembled, open, he led the Duke of Medina Cœli into it.

The Duke de Mondejar rose when he heard the name, but seeing the Inquisitor leave the room with the Duke of Medina Cœli, he was so much afraid of offending Pierre Arbues, that he scarcely dared to address the daughter of his old friend. Dolores advanced towards him, and a murmur of approbation ran through the assembly at her appearance.

"My lord," said Dolores, who had noticed the confusion of the duke, "is the presence of a fugitive so dangerous to you that she must change the happiness of this assembly into sadness?"

The duke pointed to a chair, but made no answer; all were silent, and looking on with intense anxiety; Mondejar was affected by the appearance of the poor girl, but his father-in-law and the Grand Inquisitor could hear all that was said from the place where they were concealed. At length, Dolores again gathered courage.

"My lord," she said, "my father groans in the dungeons of the Inquisition; he was once your friend, my lord, and you well know the purity of his faith. Oh! let the evidence of one of the best of Christians avail him in his miserable situation : restore my father to me and I will bless you!"

At this instant a harsh and chilling laugh issued from the adjoining cabinet, and Pierre Arbues made his appearance. At the sight of her persecutor, Dolores uttered a loud scream and fainted. The Duke de Mondejar, pale and terrified, knew not how to act, but the Inquisitor gave him a peculiar look, and the duke appeared to recover himself; he rang and two attendants made their appearance.

"Let this young woman be taken to her own home in my litter."

The attendants obeyed and carried out the governor's daughter in their arms, for she was still insensible. The duke also went out by another door, and at the end of some minutes he returned with a smiling countenance.

"Duke de Mondejar," said the Inquisitor, "when Heaven calls the Duke de Medina-Cœli to its bosom, you shall succeed him as grand standard-bearer."

*   *   *   *   *   *

In the prison of the Holy Office at Seville there is an apartment known as the "Chamber of Mercy;" if a very rich personage is accused, he in the first instance inhabits this room, from which he has on some occasions been released by making over the whole of his property to the Inquisition.

The closed litter that left the mansion of the Duke de Mondejar passed along the street of the Inquisition, and did not stop until it reached the palace. One of the men who accompanied the litter knocked at the door, and the porter opened it. The valet immediately whispered a few words in his ear, and both of them proceeding to the litter, they lifted the fainting girl out of it, and conveyed her to the Chamber of Mercy; there they placed her on a bed, and carefully locking the door, again descended the stairs.

" Teresa," said the porter to his wife, " go up stairs, and see how the senora gets on ; she seems more dead than alive."

The woman, who was half an idiot, did as she was ordered, and, seating herself silently near the young girl, she waited until Heaven should restore her to life. Three hours passed before the fit had left her, and then stretching out her arms and opening her eyes, she looked around her with an air of astonishment, for she had no recollection of the room or the furniture.

" Juana," she cried, in a soft and melancholy voice.

" My name is not Juana," said the idiot by her bedside, " my name is Teresa."

The young girl looked at the woman, and, not recognising her, she uttered a fearful scream.

" Where am I then ?" she exclaimed.

" In prison," said the foolish creature.

" In prison ! in prison ! What have I done to be placed in prison ?"

" That I don't know ; it's no business of mine."

" Oh, my God !" cried Dolores, " what has happened to-day ; and why am I now here ? Ah ! yes ; I remember, when I left Juana's house every one was merry—I alone was oppressed by despair. I went to my father's friends—I surprised them in the midst of their feasting—I prayed and wept, and begged of them to restore my father to me—they would not listen to me ; and there, concealed like a traitor, the Grand Inquisitor overheard my words—they gave me up to the executioner, and in the house of this noble duke I did not even meet with the safeguard of hospitality ; my life has been sacrificed for a smile from Pierre Arbues." Then addressing the porter's wife, she said, " What is the time ?"

" I do not know, senora, but it has been night a long while ; I was asleep when you arrived, for I was very weary. There has been a fête to-day, and so many prisoners have come in."

Dolores had not deceived herself ; a most cowardly act of perfidy had placed her in the power of the Inquisitor. The order given aloud by the Duke de Mondejar was merely intended to deceive the guests ; instead of acting like a honourable man, he had yielded to the dictates of the Inquisitor ; and yet he was neither a cowardly soldier, a bad nobleman, nor a false friend—he was simply a man who dreaded the power of the Inquisition.

Dolores was overcome beneath the load of the dreadful certainty—she was no longer free. Oppressed with sorrow, her head drooping on her chest, she was overwhelmed with the dreadful idea ; then suddenly her wild despair returned, and she burst out into a fit of heartbreaking cries and convulsive sobs.

The porteress arose, terrified at this painful demonstration of grief.

" Senora," she said, " do not weep so much ; they have given you the handsomest chamber in the prison of the Inquisition."

At that dreadful word the governor's daughter started convulsively on the bed ; her sobs were hushed ; her terror had become so great she could neither sigh nor complain.

" Senora," said her gaoler, " since you are not dead, you have no further need of me ; I will go and sleep," and she left the room.

While the unfortunate girl was thus left alone a prey to grief and terror, José and the Grand Inquisitor were together in the palace. José was turning over the leaves of a Latin Bible, overcome by some sad presentiment; but as yet he was ingorant that Dolores was in the power of the Inquisition. The last repast of the evening was over; but although it was already past midnight Pierre Arbues could not resolve to postpone the pleasure of seeing Dolores until the morrow: he was waiting for José to retire; but the latter, like a true favourite, perceiving that his presence annoyed his master, persisted in keeping his eyes fixed on his Bible, of which he did not read a word.

At length Pierre Arbues, losing patience, approached him, smiling.

" Come, my little José, leave off your reading; I wish to sleep, and you also must be weary; you look as pale as a girl the day after a ball."

" And yet, I assure your eminence, I am not in the least fatigued."

" Your zeal is great, my good José; and when the death of Alphonso Manrique allows me to aspire to the office of Inquisitor General, I hope to see you appointed Grand Inquisitor of Seville."

" I do not wish it, if it would be necessary I should leave your eminence; but I think, my lord, I begin to feel, like you, rather sleepy—deign to give me your blessing, and I will retire immediately;" and he bent his head before the Inquisitor.

Pierre Arbues extended his arms, and, having pronounced his benediction, he added—" To-morrow, my child, come to me before the hour appointed for the question;" and he left the room by a door leading to his sleeping apartment, and thence, descending a private staircase, he reached the street.

Instead of retiring to his own room, José proceeded to the court-yard of the palace, and concealed himself behind an oleander-tree. It was about the hour when Pierre Arbues was accustomed to leave the palace with four familiars; usually José accompanied the Inquisitor in these mysterious excursions, and the young monk was anxious to know whither he was going without his company.

Pierre Arbues soon made his appearance, the four familiars following at a distance; scarcely had the palace-gates closed upon them when José gently opened the door, and glided after them. They directed their course to the street of the Inquisition, and the Inquisitor, having knocked at the door, was admitted without delay; the place was dark, and José, close at his heels, followed gently after him, at the risk of being discovered. But Pierre Arbues thought little of him; he darted up the staircase that led to the first floor, and as José was in the habit of following him, the gaoler let him pass without question; then safely closing the gate, he took up his lantern and bunch of keys, ready to attend on the Inquisitor. The young Dominican seated himself on a bench in the corridor, and the familiars remained without.

The gaoler soon redescended the stairs, and taking no heed of José, entered his lodge, and laid himself down to sleep. Then José in his turn ascended the stairs, and as he had heard a door open and shut again, he stopped on the first landing-place, thinking he should be able to discover the secret of which he was in search. He had crept cautiously a few paces only along the corridor when he perceived a ray of light issuing from the keyhole of one of the apartments, and at the same time he heard two voices which he could not mistake—one belonged to the Inquisitor, and the other to Dolores. He shuddered with terror at the sound of the well-known accents, but he could not comprehend by what fatality Dolores had been removed from the retreat he had provided for her. Seized with mortal anxiety, he endeavoured, by looking through the keyhole, to see what was going on within the apartment, but the key, which had been left in the lock, prevented his seeing anything distinctly. He listened attentively. Meanwhile the following scene was taking place within the chamber :—

At the instant Pierre Arbues entered the apartment, the governor's daughter was reclining on the bed, her face buried in the pillow. Wearied out by a night and day so replete with terror and anguish, she had yielded to weariness, and fallen into a slight doze ; thus, resting on the pure white bedding, from which her black dress stood out in relief, the maiden looked inexpressibly interesting and graceful. Seeing her thus more beautiful in her grief than she had ever appeared in her prosperity, the Inquisitor stood still, trembling as if he were about to commit a sacrilegious act. He looked around with a terrified air, as if he wished to satisfy himself there was no invisible witness in the air ready to accuse him. The deepest silence reigned through the chamber, and nothing was heard but the gentle breathing of the sleeping girl. Pierre Arbues suppressed with difficulty the importunate fear that assailed him. " I am mad," he said to himself; and he seated himself in an arm-chair near the head of the bed. Dolores still slept. Pierre Arbues had time to gaze on her for a few minutes, and recover his self-possession. The vague terror with which he had been overtaken gave way to a burst of frenzied passion ; but still, notwithstanding his audacity and certain impunity, he dared not commit the crime with all its horrors, and this internal struggle saved the governor's daughter.

We have said she slept but gently. The Inquisitor, plunged in deep ecstacy, gazed upon her, but dared not awaken her; in his delirium he bent over the hand that rested on the pillow, and impressed his burning lips upon it. Dolores shuddered at the touch, and, half opening her heavy eyes, she uttered a cry of terror and buried her face in her hands at the sight of the dark form seated before her.

" Do you fear me, then ?" said the Inquisitor, in a gentle tone.

" Oh ! my lord, why do you pursue me thus ?" she said, in broken accents.

" My daughter," replied Pierre Arbues, reassuming the character of an Inquisitor, " the shepherd always seeks the sheep that has strayed, until he finds it."

" The wolf also seeks the sheep that he may devour it."

" Dolores," said the worthy disciple of Dominic de Guzman, irritated at the failure of his hypocrisy, " Dolores, I see with sorrow that your mind is blinded and perverted by the abominable doctrines of reform ; whoever trusts in Heaven trusts in its ministers, and you put no trust in me. Know you not that we punish the perishable body to save the immortal soul ?"

"Alas! my lord, if these are the means you employ for the salvation of souls, renounce them quickly; they only answer the purpose of causing the justice of Heaven to be doubted."

"Dolores," at length said the Inquisitor, mildly, "you wish not to be converted?"

"I am a Christian in heart and soul, my lord; why do you persecute me?"

"Child, how you abuse my real sentiments," said Pierre Arbues, drawing close to the young girl, while she drew around her her silken petticoat that touched the Inquisitor's robe.

"Oh! mercy, mercy! my lord," she cried, clasping her hands; "give me back my father—my liberty!"

"It depends on you," he continued, looking on her with passionate admiration.

Dolores trembled and turned pale; she remembered the scene that took place a few months previously in her oratory, and she was now in the Inquisitor's power.

José heard the whole of this conversation; but as he pressed his ear close to the keyhole, that he might not lose a single word, the door gave way a little, and he found it had not been closed; he drew back, therefore, that he might not open it further, happy at having made the discovery.

"Oh! Dolores," continued the Inquisitor, "you cannot imagine how burthensome and wearisome a task it is to guide mankind, and lead them into the right way; but Heaven in its goodness sometimes prepares us for unexpected consolation. There are select souls—such as yours, for instance—on whom we are permitted to bestow not only spiritual affection, but even terrestrial love, without offence to Heaven."

"Can it be possible," said Dolores to herself, "that he has the good of Heaven in view?"

She almost ceased to look on the Inquisitor with distrust.

"My lord," she said, "what interest can you have in deceiving a poor girl? If you think I am in error, teach me better. I will practise the doctrine you teach; but oh! restore my father!"

"Dolores," cried the Inquisitor, triumphantly, "my beautiful Dolores, I like to see you thus docile and charming! Yes; I will restore your father to you, and I will grant you your liberty. Oh! what woman shall be happier or more beloved?" and he rose, and fixed his dark eye upon the maiden; he spoke not, but his chest heaved violently, and the candour of the young girl alone restrained his unbridled passion.

For a few seconds he remained standing, alarmed, and not daring to commit a fresh crime: his former victims passed before him in imagination as in a dream, crying and shouting, and calling for vengeance!—vengeance sounded in his ears like the bell of an alarum; but soon his sight became indistinct, and like a man who, seized with giddiness, plunges headlong into an abyss, the Inquisitor stretched out his arms, and sprang forwards towards the motionless girl.

"It must be so," he cried, in a hollow tone.

Dolores screamed loudly.

"My lord!" said José, opening the door of the prison room.

Pierre Arbues, restored to himself by this sudden apparition, raised his head proudly, and in an angry tone said,

"What is it you have come here for?"

"I came, my lord, to endeavour to convert several heretics."

"Are you tired of your life that you thus throw yourself in my way?"

"My lord misunderstands the zeal of his faithful servant," returned the favourite in a humble tone; "but the servant has nothing to dread from so good a master, and José, the Inquisitor, has no fear of the Inquisition."

Dolores looked with surprise on the young Dominican; but he enjoined her by a look not to recognise him.

"Go!" said the Inquisitor imperiously.

"I do not leave without your eminence: the rumour of a riot is circulated in the town, and they speak of a conspiracy against your precious life."

"Indeed," observed the Inquisitor, rather alarmed.

"It is very true, my lord: I will accompany you therefore; for," he added, showing a slender poniard, which he carried in his scapulary, "in case of necessity, this good Toledo blade might defend your eminence; it is an excellent weapon, my lord; it will never deceive its master! Come, then, my lord, and fear nothing."

Pierre Arbues, in spite of himself, yielded to the influence of José; and, then, approaching Dolores, he said gently to her,

"To-morrow, I trust, I shall find you with more humbled feelings, daughter."

"I hate you!" she exclaimed, turning aside in disgust. "Let me die with my father, it is the only favour I ask of you!"

José drew the Inquisitor after him.

"Oh! let me be avenged on her!" cried Arbues, grinding his teeth with rage. "What can I do to crush her indomitable spirit?"

"My lord," said José, "send her to the chamber of penitence."

CHAPTER XIX.

THE TORTURE BY WATER.

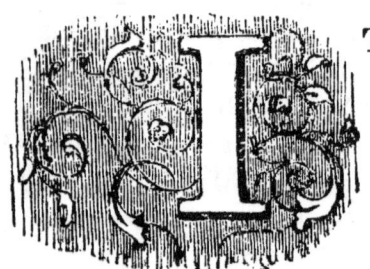

IT would be difficult to give a correct idea of the rage and disappointment of the Grand Inquisitor, when he saw his most secret and best laid plot fail through some fatality, he even looked suspiciously on his favourite, José; but he remembered it was the day appointed for the question: the auto-da-fé was drawing near, and a great number of the accused had to figure in a scene of his long and horrible drama that lasted for three centuries.

José, with his usual confidence, entered the Inquisitor's apartment before he had left his bed, where we lay wearied out by a sleepless night. At the sight of his favourite, Pierre Arbues knit his brows; but the young Dominican was unmoved.

"Has my lord any commands?" he said, in that gentle and submissive tone whose accents were irresistible.

"Your audacity is really astonishing after last night's occurrence; how dare you come into my presence?"

"My lord desired me to come before the hour appointed for the question," said the favourite, humbly.

The tone of José's words produced the effect he expected, for in the hands of this youth the surly Arbues was like softened wax.

"I am ready for you," said Pierre Arbues, as if he had taken some sudden resolution. "Come, do not let the torturers await our coming. How many are there for the question to-day?" and as if he wished to stifle his rage in the horrible delights of torture, he reckoned over in a loud voice the names of the victims; like a tiger in the arena, he enjoyed by anticipation the agonies of the prey he was about to devour. In a few minutes he was ready. "Come, my son," he said to José, "let our zeal in the cause of Heaven console us for the deception of this earth, and make us worthy of its protection."

When they arrived at the prison, the corridors were thronged; two torturers, clothed in their dismal costume, were flogging and driving before them six prisoners, among whom were three women. One of the three, young, tall, and handsome, although marked by the sufferings of her imprisonment, had a gag between her ivory teeth, which prevented her crying out. These unfortunate creatures were naked to the waist, women as well as men, their shoulders scourged by the whip, were covered with violet-coloured marks; but, notwithstanding their frightful punishment they uttered not the least complaint. The Inquisitor passed before them without the appearance of the slightest emotion, but José shuddered inwardly. The woman who was gagged walked last; when she came opposite Pierre Arbues she looked fixedly at him, and, unable to speak, her black, sombre, and terrible eyes, still larger in appearance on account of her pale meagre features, her eyes full of hatred, despair, and vengeance, were fixed on those of the Inquisitor, as if they wished to say—"Do you not recollect me?"

In fact, Pierre Arbues remembered her, in spite of the dreadful change in her features. "Frances," he murmured, in a low tone, dropping his eyes before her fearful glance. The Abbess of the Carmelites was unable to speak, but she raised her eyes to heaven, as if summoning her executioner before the tribunal of the Great Judge. The Inquisitor passed on, and the executioners continued their punishment. But Pierre Arbues was about to witness a spectacle much more exciting and fertile in sensations than the miserable ceremony of the whip.

When they descended into the torture chamber, the sbirri brought before them a young and charming woman, but dreadfully pale, and so weak and ill that she could scarcely support herself; her dull and lustreless eye, of angelic softness, seemed to beg for mercy of them; and

XIV.

when she was in the presence of the Inquisitor, she made an effort to clasp her slender hands, so pale and almost transparent.

"My child," she murmured, in an almost inarticulate voice.

"My daughter," said the Inquisitor, in the gentle tone he knew how to assume, "your sister is a Lutheran, and you are accused of having encouraged her in her apostacy.

"It is false! it is false!" replied the unhappy woman, with all the energy she possessed.

"Have you nothing to say to support your denial?"

"My child! give me back my child!" repeated the unfortunate creature, in heart-rending accents.

The child she called for with so much anguish was scarcely eight days old, and the poor mother, imprisoned before it was born, was put to the question shortly after its birth, as her mangled wrists attested.

Neither her tears nor prayers, sufficient to have moved a rock, had any effect on the pitiless Arbues; José alone concealed in his bosom a deep and terrible emotion, and it required all the firmness years of dissimulation had taught him to avoid sobbing aloud and cursing the Inquisitor; but Arbues made a sign, and the torturers seized their victim. There was no necessity to give orders, they well knew what to do; it was the second time she had undergone the question. Two athletic men brought in a chevalet, and placed it in the centre of the chamber. This horrible wooden instrument was formed like a gutter, and large enough to receive the body of a man; the bottom consisted of a piece of carved wood, round which the body was bent, so that the head of the sufferer was lower than the feet. The torturers lifted up the half-dead woman, and tied her limbs with cords, and the victim submitted without uttering a complaint; but the Inquisitor approached her to induce her to confess to the crime of which she was accused. The unfortunate creature again protested her innocence in as loud a voice as her strength would permit.

"Impenitent! impenitent!" cried the Grand Inquisitor, sadly.

At these words the two men violently turned a winch, which tightened the cords with which the victim was bound, and mangled her flesh so sadly that the blood spirted out even over the executioners. The unfortunate creature uttered a cry of agony, as if her power of suffering had been that instant resumed. The torturers coolly wiped the blood from their dress with their large black sleeves. Pierre Arbues again drew near.

"Confess, my sister," he said, in gentle accents.

The poor creature was too weak to speak, but she made a negative sign; in the position in which she was placed she could scarcely breathe.

"Impenitent!" repeated the Inquisitor.

The torturers placed over the face of the sufferer a piece of very fine linen soaked in water, one part of which was forced to the bottom of her throat, and the other covered her nostrils; then they slowly poured water into her throat and nose; the water filtered drop by drop through the wet cloth, and as it was introduced into her throat and nostrils her respiration became more difficult, and she made the most strenuous efforts to swallow the water and breathe a little air, but at each of these attempts, which necessarily was accompanied by a violent convulsive effort, the torturers turned the winch, and the cord penetrated her very sinews. It was horrible! For more than an hour the torturers thus continued to pour water into the throat of the sufferer, restoring her to animation at intervals by drawing the cords more tightly round her limbs. At each turn of the winch the miserable creature uttered a cry, weaker and weaker still—a cry of inexpressible agony. At length the cry became so faint that the physician of the Inquisition, having felt her pulse, turned towards the Grand Inquisitor, and said—

" My lord, this woman can endure no more without dying."

" Release her," said Pierre Arbues; " the question is suspended until fresh orders."

The tormentors then removed the linen that covered her face, but when they had loosened one of the cords with which her slender limbs were bound, they perceived that the flesh had been cut to the very bone. José went up to the victim with inexpressible horror, and having examined her features, he said—

" My lord, this woman is dead."

" Do you think so?" observed the Inquisitor; and at the same time, the torturers having placed her in an upright position, the unfortunate creature was seized with a convulsive cough, while streams of black blood escaped from her mouth; then, without opening her eyes, she murmured, " My child!" and expired.

" May Heaven have mercy on her!" said Pierre Arbues.

" Suppose this woman should have been innocent," observed José, in a whisper.

" Then she is in heaven. Why do you lament her death?"

Two attendants removed the corpse, and another victim appeared before his eminence. It was an old and worthy woman, whose head had blanched in the exercise of the sublimest charity: it was the noble Marie de Bourgogne, called the " mother of the poor," accused by her discharged servant of having uttered the words, " The Christians have neither faith nor law."

Marie was ninety years old, and at that age it was against the rule to apply the torture; she had already been subjected to the water torture and that of the cord. Her immense wealth had attracted notice, and she was accused of holding Jewish doctrines.

" Sister," said the Inquisitor, mildly, " will you confess your crime, and obtain pardon?"

" Whatever may become of me," replied the " mother of the poor," proudly, " I am innocent."

" Proceed," said the Inquisitor, pointing to the burning brazier in the corner.

" Pierre Arbues," cried the old woman, in an inspired tone, " you are accursed by Him who came on the earth to bless it!"

" A Jewess! a Jewess!" exclaimed the sbirri, crossing themselves in terror; and while they uttered these words they stripped the old woman of her garments, one by one, and when she was almost entirely naked, they wished to carry her in their arms, but she thrust them back with a dignified air.

"I will walk," she said; "where am I to go?"

They pointed to the brazier in the corner of the dungeon.

Marie, with a firm step, moved towards it, and looked without apparent emotion at the flaming gulf before her. The tormentors laid their patient on a wooden bench by the side of the brazier, and bound her firmly to it by means of cords. She allowed them to do so without resistance; then, giving a rotatory movement to the bench, they placed it in such a position that one of the extremities—that on which the feet of the victim rested—almost touched the glowing coals.

When she first felt the fire Marie de Burgogne gave a deep sigh, the only expression of pain she uttered during her horrible punishment.

"We have forgotten something," said one of the executioners, suddenly, when he saw the feet of the victim become excessively red, and then grow white like burning parchment.

"True," replied his companion, "I did not think of it;" and he went to a corner and fetched a small earthen vessel filled with oil, and by means of a sponge placed at the end of a stick, he rubbed the sufferer's feet; the action of the fire, increased by the presence of the oil, became so penetrating that the skin cracked, and, the flesh shrinking, exposed to view the tendons and bones.

To this incredible punishment Marie opposed the most heroic firmness, until the intolerable pain drew forth an involuntary complaint; and when she was carried back to her dungeon, she had strength enough left to say to Pierre—

"May God pardon you as I do, my lord!"

The deposition of a single witness had caused Marie de Bourgogne to be condemned to death, and this witness was a slave; but Marie was too rich to meet with pity from the holy office.

José, overcome by his feelings, could scarcely stand, and approaching the ear of the Inquisitor, he said—

"My lord, I feel myself quite ill; the fumes of the charcoal give me giddiness in the head, and I feel so faint I shall die."

"You must get accustomed to that," replied Pierre Arbues; "one more torture and all will be over."

When he finished speaking, the sbirri entered the chamber.

"My lord," they said, hesitatingly.

"Well, what's the matter? speak out!"

"My lord, the prisoner is dead."

"Dead!"

"She cut her throat with her scissors."

"Why did you leave them with her?" said the Inquisitor sharply; and then the hypocritical monk exclaimed, in accents of despair, "Impenitent! she died impenitent! All prayers for the deceased would be useless; her soul belongs to the demon."

Thus ended the *sceance;* and the Inquisitor, with his favorite, left the palace.

"You are really as weak as a woman," said Pierre Arbues, in a gentle voice.

"No, my lord, I have really all the courage of a man," replied the young monk very seriously.

"We shall see that when you are put to the proof," continued the Inquisitor.

"Oh, we shall see it when the time arrives, my lord, be sure of that."

CHAPTER XX.

THE CONSPIRACY.

 SHORT distance from Seville, near the house of the apostle, a kind of cavern had been excavated out of the rock, at the foot of a woody knoll that overhung the river. The entrance to this grotto, which was almost circular, and about the height of a man, looked like a coronet of flowers.

It was night, and the cathedral clock had just struck ten. In one of the corners of this grotto a man and woman were seated on a straw mat, and near to the entrance, in another corner, a blazing wood fire cast its light on the inmates. The woman was young and well made, and gracefully seated on the mat; the man was lying down, and rested his left arm, which supported his heavy head, on his companion's knee; he preserved a profound silence, the looks and attitude of these two persons was in perfect harmony with the melancholy solitude of their dwelling. Manofina and his companion, the serena, for it was our old friends, since they had ceased to be gardunas had almost become hermits.

While thus seated in moody silence, Manofina lamenting the inactive life he led, a gush of air from without made the fire burn more briskly, and the branches that closed the entrance to the cavern were slowly put on one side.

"Who's there?" cried the guapo, rising and placing his hand on his dagger.

"Do you want to put me out of the way, brother?" said the new comer.

"By the Virgin of Carmen!" observed the serena, "who would have thought of receiving a visit from Coco, at this time of night?"

"Are you in want of our services?" added Manofina, in a cheerful tone.

"That's right, Manofina; always the same, my fine fellow. You have not lost your courage, although you have become a hermit."

"It is a long time," sighed the guapo, "since I have been told that. How happy you are, Coco," he continued; "you come and go, and you work, and, in fact, you are fit for anything, while here am I."

"What is there new in Seville?" said Culervina, trying to change the conversation.

"Oh, many things," replied the alguazil, with a mysterious look; "but I must tell you, Manofina, the society of the garduna have not yet replaced you?"

"I can well believe that," said the serena, vainly; "did they expect to do so."

"But," continued Coco, "the society is still flourishing; the Inquisitors pay them to assassinate heretics, and the heretics wish to pay them to assas——no, to carry off the inquisitors. Oh, my friend, if you did but know what is going on, the Governor of Seville is to be burnt, and his daughter imprisoned for life."

"Jesu, Maria!" cried the serena, "and what's become of Don Estevan?"

"Silence! we must not speak of him, or perhaps they will put him in prison also; but to continue, Don Estevan de Vargas who wishes at all risks to save his father-in-law and his bride, has resolved to carry off the governor and Donna Dolores on the day of the auto-da-fé, and to seize upon the inquisitors."

"I am ready!" exclaimed Manofina.

"Listen! you cannot do this alone, on which account the society of the garduna must have half the duty to perform, if we would be successful: I know you do not now belong to the society; but the master has not been able to supply your place; and, on the other hand, we must have the assistance of the master to carry out our plot. So you must go and seek him. You were always a favorite, and he will not refuse if you promise to make one. He will do this the rather in the hopes of your again entering the society."

"But," replied Manofina, "if I allow him to think so, I shall be deceiving him."

"Not in the least; you make no promise and break none. Then Don Estevan is rich, and I think the reward I am authorised to offer will be well worth the trouble. Come, let us be off."

The guapo remained for an instant overpowered by his different emotions, while the serena anxiously waited the decision of her lord and master. At length he sprang up like a wild bull, and girding himself with the red belt, in which he carried his dagger, he exclaimed in a loud voice—

"Come on!"

The serena, as light as a mountain goat, was instantly at his side, and they all three left the cavern.

As they were about to pass the exterior walls of the palace of the garduna, they were delighted with the spectacle that met their eyes, a gush of light streamed from the half-open door, and the sound of a guitar and of singing were heard.

"Let us go in," said the serena, whose impatient little feet were moving in cadence to the music, for she was the best dancer of the fandango in Seville. They hastened forward, and as they passed a thicket of trees they could just discern in the gloom three men, whom they could not recognise by their dress or appearance. They were talking to each other in a whisper; but, notwithstanding their impatience, a feeling of pride, when about to cross the threshold of the place they had abandoned, made them hesitate.

"Well, go in," said the alguazil.

"No, you go, Coco; you must introduce us," said the serena.

"Well, then, if it must be so, we'll go in together; and as to you, Manofina, you will soon see whether I am well received;" and Coco opened the door to its full width, and marched proudly into the midst of the assembly, Manofina following at a short distance.

"Heaven protect your lordships," said the alguazil.

An expression of astonishment was heard through the assembly when they recognised the new comers, and all were anxious to know what had brought them back. The room was well lighted, and the women seated round, each occupying a separate mat; while the men, lounging on the ground, rested their elbow on the knees of their partners. The master himself advanced when he saw them, and assuming his most gracious smile, said courteously—

"What saint in Paradise, my girl, induced you to come here? You are welcome, and Manofina also," he said, extending his huge hand.

A loud hurrah of congratulation followed this hearty reception, and they all gathered round their ancient companions.

"I suppose, my children," said the master, at length, "Manofina's presence has some motive. Is he in any danger, and does he need our assistance? Although no longer one of us, we are always willing to assist a friend."

"Brother Mandamiento," replied Coco, "Manofina's safety is not in question; on the contrary, we must try to get him to help us. I have to propose a job to you of the most serious nature, and that is why I have brought Manofina with me. There is a young lord in Seville in need of your assistance."

"I am always proud to assist young lords. To put a rival out of the the way, perhaps?"

"No, something you never yet attempted. It is to assist in rescuing the Governor of Seville during the auto-da-fé."

"What!"

"Carrying off the Grand Inquisitor, and keeping him prisoner two days will enable Don Estevan to quit Spain."

"Do you know what you ask, brother?" said the master, terrified.

"Against two hundred thousand réals, which Don Estevan will give you as a reward."

"Two hundred thousand réals—two hundred——"

"Yes, to carry off my lord Arbues, and keep him two days in the vaults of the garduna."

"And after my lord Arbues is free," replied the master, "he will have us all burnt as heretics. Do you think I am an idiot, Coco? Kill him, if you like—the dead can do us no harm; but carry him off—no; I only carry off young girls."

"His lordship does not wish him to be killed."

"His lordship is as gentle as a lamb. If it had not been for Manofina and the orders of——. But enough; I understand. If Don Estevan is still living, it is not the Inquisitor's fault."

"I care but little about the Inquisitor's life," said Coco; "but if you talk about slaying him to Don Estevan he will never consent, and the Governor of Seville will be burned."

"Good, good, I will be discreet," replied Mandamiento, with a fiendish laugh. Two hundred thousand réals," thought he to himself, "to have the pleasure of stabbing this accursed Inquisitor, who, since I failed in the case of Don Estevan, has not brought me a single job—two hundred thousand réals." Then, addressing Coco, he said, "Does Manofina agree to be one in the business?"

"Certainly," replied the guapo, quickly.

"Well, then," said Coco, "is it a bargain, master? May I bring Don Estevan and his friends here, that you may talk together, and arrange the matter?"

"You may," replied the master, well pleased at the promised assistance of Manofina.

In the meantime Coco left the palace, and directed his steps towards the thicket of trees, where the three men we have noticed were in conversation; they were still there, as if expecting some one. The alguazil, as he advanced, intentionally made a slight noise. Don Estevan turned round, and recognised him.

"Well?" he said.

"All is ready, sir knight; the master of the garduna will do all you wish?"

"I told you so," said Estevan, addressing his two companions, two noblemen who had joined him in the plot; "now we are sure of success."

"Follow me, gentlemen," said Coco; "enter the ball-room without ceremony, that we may avoid suspicion. Amuse yourselves, and chatter with the girls."

The alguazil first entered, and at that moment all was lively and animated; a merry bolero, danced by Manofina and the serena, attracted the attention of all. The serena, with outstretched neck, moist and sparkling eyes, her little hands armed with castanets, twined herself like a snake, balancing her lissome form with the utmost grace. The guapo, animated by the music and the roguish glances of Culervina, and also by the applause of the assembly, exhibited his skill and vigour in the bustling dance. When they had ended, a loud and long-continued hurrah rang through the hall, and at that instant the three noblemen entered. Coco went up to the master, and pointing to Don Estevan de Vargas, observed—

"That is the young lord who pays."

"The same that Manofina was to have stabbed," observed Mandamiento; "there appears to be war to the death between this young lord and the Inquisitor of Seville. Well, Coco, let them remain; after the fête we will speak; but the gardunos at present want their suppers;" and the viands were immediately placed on a long mat, spread out upon the ground, and they all fell to at once, eating heartily, and making their ten fingers answer the purpose of forks.

The supper disappeared with marvellous rapidity, and all were merry, including the new comers. No one would have suspected that a plot was concealed beneath this assumed gaiety. But as soon as Mandamiento saw that the repast was ended, he made a sign, and all the gardunos, men and women, arose at once, and, leaving the room, they proceeded each to the post assigned to them before the repast, and no one remained in the Garduna, excepting the master, the alguazil, Manofina and his partner, and the three noblemen.

The master opened a great oaken chest that rested in one of the corners of the room, and drew from it a parchment account-book, yellow and dirty, a small leaden cup containing ink, and a large eagle's feather rudely formed into a pen; he closed the chest, which answered the purpose of a desk and a table, and having placed the different objects on the lid, he went to the door to be satisfied all was safe; but at the same instant José entered the room—he had been informed of the meeting by Coco.

At the sight of the young Dominican, Estevan uttered a cry of rage; and, turning towards the alguazil, he exclaimed, in an under tone—

"You have deceived me, villain !"

"No, my lord," replied the latter, coolly; "I have not deceived you."

"What does your reverence wish for?" said the master to José, a little alarmed.

"To speak to these three gentlemen," replied José; and approaching Estevan he held out his hand amicably.

Estevan did not take it; but looking him steadily in the face, he said—

"Is it not enough to have betrayed me, but you would also destroy me ?"

"I have not betrayed you, and I come to comfort and assist you."

"But Dolores—what have you done with her ?"

"Dolores shall be restored to you, safe and sound."

For the second time since he had known José, Don Estevan was overcome by the simplicity and truth, and the attractive charm that breathed through the features of the young monk; he held out his hand in his turn in a frank and friendly manner, but still a cruel doubt beset him, and, after a little hesitation, he said—

"One thing further. If you would convince me, restore to me Dolores and her father; José, the favourite of the Inquisitor, can do anything in the Holy Office."

"José can do much," replied the favourite; "but he cannot restore a man whose limbs are broken and seared."

"What say you ?"

"That Don Manuel d'Argoso was subjected yesterday to the question of fire and water, and he cannot escape, for he is unable to walk: as to Dolores, be tranquil; she has endured no torture, and I will deliver her. If after the auto-da-fé you do not find her in Juana's house, do what you please to me, Don Estevan."

"Swear to restore Dolores to me."

"Oaths were invented for rogues; I promise you."

XV.—XVI.

"Come, gentlemen, to business," exclaimed Estevan; "the deliverance of Don Manuel d'Argoso must be effected, if we perish in the attempt; and here Heaven has sent us assistance," and he pointed to José. "And now, master," he continued, turning to Mandamiento, "are you ready to place all your forces at my disposal?"

"That depends upon circumstances," replied the master; "our forces will be in larger or smaller numbers, according to the necessity of the case, and the amount paid to the brotherhood."

"The payment is of no moment; you shall be handsomely paid. Are not two hundred thousand réals enough, master; and cannot you bring into the field three or four hundred persons for that sum?"

"It may be done, sir knight; but you must add twenty thousand réals for travelling expenses, for I shall be obliged to send for some of our fraternity from the neighbouring towns."

"I will give the twenty thousand réals," said Don Ximenes de Herrera, one of Estevan's companions.

"In that case will your lordships give me the promise in writing, and I will enter the order in the registry of our fraternity. Write, sir knight," he continued; and Estevan wrote a promise to pay the sum of two hundred and twenty thousand réals the day before the auto-da-fé on the next 4th of June.

"Enough, gentlemen; and now to make a note of your demand;" upon which, Mandamiento, with a serious and business-like air, took down his instructions; according to which, he was to provide a certain number of guapos for the purpose of "assassinating the Grand Inquisitor," wrote Mandamiento.

"Strike that out," exclaimed Estevan; "you are to carry him off only—no murder, Mandamiento."

The master pretended to erase the word with his pen, but he had taken care previously to wipe out the ink on his jacket.

"You are to carry him to the caverns that lie beneath your rendezvous, and place him afterwards in the hands of Father José or myself."

"Is that all?" observed Mandamiento.

"All; but you must omit nothing to ensure the success of our enterprise."

"My lord," replied the captain, vainly, "do you consider the honour and reputation we should lose in case of failure as nothing?"

At that instant a knock was heard at the door—everyone started; but Mandamiento, without being alarmed, pushed on one side a moveable column, and pointed to a badly-lighted room; it was his own apartment. "All of you go in." They obeyed; and having replaced the column, he opened the door. It was La Chapa, who rushed into the room in a state of great distress.

"What is the matter, my Chapica? Is the house on fire?"

"Where is my brother?" she exclaimed, eagerly; and the master opened the door of his apartment.

"Gentlemen, there is no danger; you may come out."

"Oh! gentlemen," exclaimed the terrified girl, "if you did but know what a misfortune has happened," and, suffocated with her tears, she was unable to proceed. At length recovering herself, she sobbed forth—"The apostle has been arrested by the Inquisition."

"Avenging Heaven!" exclaimed Estevan.

"Would you save the neck of the Inquisitor now, my lord?" observed the master.

"Mandamiento," returned the nobleman, "your business and that of your gardunos is solely to secure the person of Pierre Arbues."

"Be satisfied, my lord; his eminence shall not escape."

And matters being thus arranged, they left the palace of the Garduna together.

CHAPTER XXI.

THE AUTO-DA-FÉ.

 T was the morning of the 4th of June, 1534; the clock had just struck four. The population had arisen before their usual time; a great event kept every mind in suspense. It was the day of the auto-da-fé— a holiday, solemn and sacred, on which none were to work, but all to pray. The streets were crowded, and bands of monks, issuing forth from houses of entertainment in which they had been carousing the whole of the night, mingled with the populace.

At this instant the procession left the palace of the Inquisition. The march was led by the faggot-bearers, at least a hundred in number, each armed with a pike or musket; then followed a large white cross, borne by two monks, in their long black and white dresses; after them, the Duke of Medina-Cœli, the hereditary standard-bearer; the nobles of Spain succeeded him, and hosts of monks and familiars.

Soon the victims appeared. At their head were those condemned to slight penances; their attitude was humble and looks downcast, for they knew that although they were spared they were condemned to infamy for the rest of their lives; behind them came those who were to be sent to the galleys, the scourge, or imprisonment; then those whose fate it was to be burnt after strangulation, the devils and flames on their *san benito* being reversed. Those who were to be burnt alive came last, and the flames on their dress were painted as if ascending; each held a taper of yellow wax in his hand; among these Manuel Argoso came the last; but, wearied out with his torture, he was obliged to be carried by two familiars.

As soon as this part of the procession appeared, the gardunos mixed with the crowd; and with Mandamiento at their head, each bearing an enormous rosary, they arranged themselves on each side of the victims, and followed the procession, praying earnestly.

The sound of horses' feet was next heard, and the Inquisitors themselves appeared, with Pierre Arbues at their head. As soon as the latter came up, Manofina, followed by his faithful Culervina, commenced humbly to walk by his side, and prayed with even more fervour than his companions. Suddenly a loud sound like the barking of a dog was heard, and the master, on whom the eyes of all the gardunos were fixed, made the sign of the cross, and kissed the medal of his rosary; while, at the signal, two of the guapos, violently thrusting on one side the familiars who carried the governor, took the old man in their arms of iron, and carried him off, while the chivatos held the familiars, and fled with the rapidity of lightning. The monks themselves threw down the crucifix, and attempted to escape; but they were prevented by the crowd. The Grand Inquisitor had seen nothing of this, when a fresh barking was heard, near to Manofina, and instantly, as swift as thought, he sprang on the crupper of Pierre Arbues' horse, and struck him with his poniard in the middle of his back; then as lightly springing down, he decamped with so rapid a step that it was impossible to see who had struck the blow. But at the instant he slipped down the back of the horse the serena suddenly seized upon one of the sbirri of the holy office, and cried out lustily—

" This is he! This is the assassin! He meant to kill the Grand Inquisitor;" and she held him in her strong little hands, to give Manofina the opportunity of escaping,

But Pierre Arbues had not even staggered in his seat, and he looked around with a triumphant smile.

" Heaven has wrought a miracle!" exclaimed the crowd, for they were ignorant that Pierre Arbues wore a cuirass beneath his dress.

The procession again continued its course. But while this was going on, the door of the house where Juana lived was opened, and José, who had left the crowd, entered the house in company with a young monk. That monk was Dolores. José had kept his promise.

While the procession was leaving the palace of the Inquisition, the Plaza Mayor became by degrees filled by the crowd. Before the house of the Duke of Medina-Cœli a scaffold had been erected, and to the right of this scaffold an amphitheatre, intended for the councillors of the different courts of Spain. Above this was placed the chair for the Grand Inquisitor. A second amphitheatre, intended for the victims, was on the left, and facing the other; in the second, and opposite the king's balcony, was a third very small balcony, on which were placed two cages, in which the condemned were confined while their sentences were being read. A number of Dominican priests, on their knees, were praying with humble fervour in the centre of the square; fifteen piles of faggots of fir timber might be counted. The place where these piles were raised was called the Quemadero.

The Emperor Charles the Fifth already occupied his place in the royal balcony, along with many richly-dressed ladies, and the places destined for the people were rapidly filled. At length the ceremony began. The condemned persons having made the circuit of the scaffold, and passed beneath the king's balcony, took their seats in the left-hand amphitheatre, the monks and the familiars remaining near them. Finally, the Grand Inquisitor mounted the steps leading to his throne, and seated himself with an air of triumphant humility. Deep silence reigned over the whole of this immense assembly, mass was celebrated, and at its conclusion the Dominician whose duty it was to preach made the sign of the cross, and began.

"My brethren," he said, "*Inquisitio superior regibus* (the Inquisition is superior to kings), for the power of heaven is above that of earth; the Inquisition is the gate of Paradise; it dates from the creation of the world and the origin of the Tower of Babel."

In this manner he continued to preach for a considerable time; and when he had concluded, the reading of the sentences commenced.

"The first two condemned persons placed in the cages were the abbess, of the Carmelites, and a man of noble blood, Herrezuelo; the latter courageous to the last, refused to listen to the exhortations of the confessor; but it was far different with Frances de Lerma: her courage failed her at the thought of her punishment, and when the reader pronounced the words " burnt alive,"

"No! no! not alive!" cried the unfortunate abbess; "I repent, and I will die a good Christian."

"Heaven be praised!" said the Grand Inquisitor, "another soul is saved."

Other prisoners were then placed in the wooden cage, among them Don Carlos de Seso, belonging to one of the first families of Italy; who, after his sentence was read, exclaimed in a loud voice, "I declare to all that I die in the religion of Luther, the true faith of the Evangelist, and not in the Roman creed, a corrupt doctrine, accommodated by the clergy to excuse their own vices."

"Let this man be gagged," exclaimed Pierre Arbues; "he scandalises the church,"

Don Carlos de Seso, forced to be silent, heard his sentence with an undaunted look.

While this was passing, ten Jewish heretics, condemned to the flames, were brought out, and each being placed against a large wooden cross, a nail was driven through their right hands. When the nail pierced their flesh, the unfortunate creatures uttered a terrible cry; but the tormentors remained unmoved: and in this condition the victims listened to their sentences.

Those who were condemned to perpetual imprisonment were next called up; at length, when the sentences were pronounced, Pierre Arbues rising from his seat gave absolution, in a loud voice, to all those who had repented. During this terrible scene, the eyes of Don José watched the proceedings with incredible attention, and at the instant the victims mounted the quemadero, a convulsive sigh escaped from his breast. The executions were about to begin, and all eyes were turned towards the scaffold, which the ten Jewish heretics mounted in the first instance; they allowed themselves to be bound with the greatest courage, and soon a thick black smoke arose around the victims.

They then led Frances de Lerma to the place where she was to be strangled, and with her, two young nuns, who had also abjured their errors, through their dread of the flames. The abbess was pale and trembling; the executioners approached the nuns and placing them on the *garrote*, bound them, and applied the circle of iron to their fair and slender necks; they then forcibly turned the screw behind the *garrote*, and their heads fell forward, while a convulsive movement agitated their frames, their eyes grew dim, their features purple, violet, and then livid; a slight rattling sound was heard, and all was over—they had ceased to suffer.

The agony of Frances was of longer duration; when the executioner placed the iron ring round her neck, the abbess, filled with sudden energy, stretched out her arms towards the amphitheatre, her dull eye for an instant recovered its animation, and sparkled with wild energy, and looking at the Inquisitor, she exclaimed—

"Unworthy priest; accursed be ———" The last word was lost, for the executioner turned the screw so violently that the victim died instantly.

Long jets of flame now rose towards heaven from the midst of clouds of smoke. The fetid odour of the burning bodies mingled with the scent of the resinous wood, and at times horrible cries and plaintive sobs issued from the midst of the sinister hecatombs, like the cries of anguish from the bowels of the infernal regions. The silence of death reigned over all; the flames by degrees expired; all was over; the night arr ved, and the memorable day was ended.

CHAPTER XXII.

DEATH AND MARRIAGE.

 HEN the two guapos carried off the governor, they quickly buried themselves in the inextricable turnings of the streets of Seville, and the people aided them so well in their flight, that before the sbirri of the Inquisition could overtake them, they were at Juana's door, which opened to receive them as if of its own accord. Estevan, Juana, and Dolores were waiting the issue of the business. The guapos, with incredible care, placed Dolores' father upon a large couch with which the room was furnished; he gave no signs of life, his arms hung useless by his side, his eyes were closed, and his face without colour, while his limbs were covered with bleeding wounds and half-healed cicatrices.

Seeing her father in this state, Dolores could not avoid giving utterance to a cry of deep sorrow; she was so pale and weak from what she had endured in prison she could not resist this last blow; she kissed her father's hand, but he returned not the filial pressure.

"Oh, Estevan!" she exclaimed, with increasing anguish, "he answers not my caresses, his hand is cold—his heart no longer beats. Estevan! Oh, tell me does my father live?"

Estevan, overcome with grief, approached slowly, and placed his hand on the heart of Argoso ; it still beat, but feebly, and at intervals.

Dolores followed all the movements of Estevan with looks of anguish, at length she said, " Well, speak Estevan ! may I hope ?"

" His heart still beats !" and Manuel Argoso slightly moved his head, and half opened his eyes.

Dolores uttered an exclamation of joy, " Oh, Estevan, he lives !"

By degrees the unfortunate governor began to recognise the objects by which he was surrounded, opened his lips, and feebly murmured, "The flames." He thought he was at the auto-da-fé. " My daughter ! Estevan ! Where am I ?

" With your friends, with your true friends," replied Dolores. " You are saved, father, and we shall soon leave Spain."

" With you, father !" said Estevan, kneeling at the old man's feet by the side of Dolores.

Seeing them thus, in spite of his extreme weakness and the pain of his mangled limbs, Manuel Argoso slowly raised both his arms, took his daughter's hand, and placed it in that of Estevan, while he murmured joyfully, " I bless you, never leave each other, and fly—fly."

" With you, with you, father ?"

" Yes ; carry my ashes with you—they will cast them to the wind. Adieu, love each other for ever !"

Manuel Argoso closed his eyes, his head fell back, and the cold hand of death arrested his voice.

Dolores uttered no complaint, dropped no tear ; she turned towards Estevan, her lips white and trembling, and said, " He will go with us ?"

" In all our wanderings," replied Estevan.

Dolores piously kissed her father's pallid brow, and drew her veil over her face.

At this instant José entered ; he saw at once what had happened, and clasped his hands with a movement of agony and disappointment. " I did all that was in my power," he said.

" I know it," returned Dolores, " and if you had been discovered your life—"

" My life," said the young monk, " What is my life to me ?"

Evening arrived, and between eleven and twelve o'clock Estevan, Dolores, and Juana arrived at Mandamiento's door ; two guapos went before as an escort, two others followed, bearing on their shoulders a large wooden coffer, carefully covered with cloth. The two first guapos knocked at the door in a preconcerted manner, the master opened it, and the whole of the party, along with the coffer, were mysteriously nt roduced into the palace of the Garduna.

Mandamiento concealed Estevan, Dolores, and Juana in the immense vaults of the palace, the coffer was exchanged for a large cedar coffin, procured by the agency of the gardunos—for no people are more devoted to your service if you pay them well.

Juana prayed with Dolores by the side of her father's remains, and John d'Avila—who had been released by the Inquisitor, so much was the rage of the populace dreaded—warned by La Chapa, had hastened to the Garduna.

It was midnight, at one extremity of the cavern a table covered with a white cloth was arranged as an altar. The deep voice of John d'Avila had an expression of profound unction, and mingled itself with the gentle accents of Don José. From time to time, the sobs that escaped from Dolores, in spite of all her efforts, broke in upon the recitative of the two monks. There was something deeply affecting in the celebration of the funeral ceremony, in the dead of the night, in this hidden place, unseen by all but themselves.

Of all those who were present Estevan, perhaps, was most sorrowful ; to his grief for the fate of his father-in-law was added his conviction of his want of power to assist his poor country ; the glory of being its liberator was not reserved for him.

At this juncture, two of the gardunos entered to carry out the coffin. Dolores saw that the last moment had arrived, and she advanced with a firm step to the funeral bed, where her father reposed, and kneeling on the bare earth, she bent her head over the body of him she loved so well, and kissed his pale forehead thrice ; then, having recovered her self possession, she went and seated herself at the farthest extremity of the cavern, and hid her face in her hands. The gardunos, with the greatest care, lifted the bier, and carried it to another cavern, still more remote, where two coberteros, having carefully disembowelled the body, placed the intestines in the coffin, which was then consigned to the earth : the body itself was embalmed by means of precious aromatics, known so well to the gipsies, and rolled up in cloth made of asbestos. The coberteros then kneeled down, and between their prayers they sprinkled the corpse with sweet perfumes, and the two guapos placed it on a grating of iron, over a large charcoal fire. As the body was consumed the cloth of asbestos became of a dazzling whiteness, and when nothing but a handful of ashes remained, the cloth and its contents were removed from the fire, and being opened, the remains of the unfortunate Governor of Seville were placed in a kind of bag, made of morocco leather, the heart itself, having been also embalmed, was placed in a silver box, and the ceremony was at an end.

While this scene was going on in one part of the palace of the Garduna, Dolores remained, wrapt in grief, in the other cavern. The apostle approached her, and speaking to her in a gentle tone of voice, she slowly raised her head.

"What else is there for me to do ?" she said.

The apostle gently took her by the hand, and assisting her to rise, led her towards Don Estevan, who advanced to meet them. John d'Avila then placed Dolores' hand in that of the young man, and said to her—

"It is the will of your father."

"And mine also," replied Dolores, with noble frankness.

Estevan took with transport the hand of his beloved José ; looked on in silence, and a species of delirium, an internal fever, seemed to consume him.

"Brother," said John d'Avila, "it is your task to bless our young friends"

"Mine !" he replied, bitterly ; "no, father, it cannot be ; let the task be yours."

"Well, be it so," replied the apostle, and he led the young couple to the altar, before which they knelt; each had on their finger a bridal-ring; they exchanged these rings, and John d'Avila blessed them, and read the marriage ceremony; they arose, and were thus united for ever.

A garduno at this instant entered the cavern, and shortly after the master himself appeared.

"Every thing is ready for you, gentleman, and two of the strongest mules await your pleasure; two of my gardunos will attend you as squires. Here is the pass-word; wherever you meet any of our brotherhood, they will allow you to pass freely or render you any assistance you may require;" and he put into Estevan's hand a piece of dirty paper on which an illegible word was scrawled.

"Where shall I meet you again, father?" said Estevan to John d'Avila.

"At Cadiz," replied the apostle; "I shall be there as soon as you."

"And you, Don José?" said Dolores, who looked on the young Dominican with sisterly affection.

"Where it shall please God," and a deep sadness seemed to come over him at parting with the young couple for whose sake he had attached himself for a short time to life.

"Gentlemen," said Mandamiento, "you must make haste, you have scarcely time to go two leagues before daylight, when you will reach the first residence of our brotherhood, there you will pass the day; for you know you can only travel at night."

They parted; and José and John d'Avila remained alone.

"Father," said José, "bless me before you go."

"My son," replied John d'Avila, more and more surprised at the manner of the young Dominican, "the Countess Estevan de Vargas was not this evening the saddest amongst us."

"Alas! no," replied José; "and now Dolores has no longer need of your assistance, pray for José, father."

"Be blessed and comforted," said the apostle, in gentle accents; and José, as if he were fearful of confiding too much, left the room quickly and directed his steps towards Juana's house.

CHAPTER XXIII.

THE INQUISITOR'S FATE.

HE young monk was alone in the room in Juana's house in which he was accustomed to pass his long and solitary day, seated on an ottoman, pale and overcome, he reclined carelessly on the cushion. Since the departure of Dolores and Estevan he had remained alone in this deserted place, and had eaten nothing for two days; and for these two days and nights he had not spoken a word, neither had he prayed. His mind was filled with a chaos of confused ideas, and at times he seemed to hold intercourse with some invisible being, who raising gently his enfeebled arms said, " Come !" but then an arm of iron would appear and oblige him to be seated again, exclaiming, " Not yet."

At length the young Dominican found his tongue, and, speaking to himself, he said, " Poor Juana! how miserable I have made thy life. Oh, that I could see you once more, and lay my head upon that bosom from which I was nourished, that I might not be alone in the world ; but I was right in removing thee from danger." (At the earnest desire of José, Juana had followed Estevan and Dolores.) " Now thou art free and my sad existence will no longer press heavily on thine. But the hour has arrived," and he rushed towards the door, and left the house never to return. It was the hour appointed for his rendezvous with Pierre Arbues. José moved quickly along, and his right hand, concealed beneath his tunic, firmly grasped the handle of his poniard. The young Dominican soon reached the church ; the odour of incense still filled the building, and a gentle light streamed through the windows of painted glass. At some little distance from a group of praying women was seen a monk kneeling before an image of the virgin and child ; from time to time he smote his breast with the greatest fervour, as if prayer had been his cherished occupation, and penitence his delight. The monk was Pierre Arbues. José remained for a few moments contemplating the man of whom he had been in search, and in spite of himself he trembled. " It is truly like him," said the young monk, " a hypocrite and rogue even with his Maker; while he prays he is thinking of fresh crimes—yes, pray, senseless monk ; utter thy last prayer—but, perhaps he repents." The inquisitor crossed himself several times, and a slight movement he made showed he was about to rise. " Oh, I must be mad," said José, " to imagine Pierre Arbues could repent ;" and recovering all his presence of mind, he advanced slowly towards the altar as if he wished to pray. At the noise he made, the Inquisitor turned round ; although pleased at the sight of José, he could not avoid starting at the expression of his countenance, and he cried out—

" What ails you ?"

José answered not, but a terrible smile sat on his pale lips. The Inquisitor drew back, thinking his favourite had lost his senses ; but before he could avoid the blow, José threw himself upon him like a tiger, and buried his poniard in his throat up to the very hilt, at a spot where the cuirass had left him unprotected. The Inquisitor stretched out his arms and fell backwards on the steps of the altar.

" You, you, José ?" he murmured as he struggled for life. José leaned over him, and said in a low voice—

" Do you remember Paula ?" At this name Pierre Arbues opened his half-closed eyes, and a terrible remembrance seemed to come over him.

" God is just !" he murmured, and then expired.

At the sight of so strange and sacrilegious a crime, the women who witnessed it uttered fearful screams and ran out of the church crying " Murder !" The whole militia of the holy office ran into the sacred building, and addressing José, whom they dared not suspect, said—

" Reverend father, do you know who is the author of this crime ?"

"I am," replied José, tranquilly, and he allowed himself to be bound without resistance, and walked slowly to the prison to which he was led.

The morning on which he was to be examined and tried, José arose betimes, and took more than ordinary care with his dress, and when the Alguazils came to remove their prisoner they remarked his radiant countenance and almost imagined a sorcerer stood before them. The tribunal before which he was led consisted of three judges, one of whom acted as president. After some preliminary questions, to which José answered with a firm voice—

"Is it you who assassinated the Grand Inquisitor of Seville?" said the president.

"It was I."

"What motive induced you to commit so great a crime?"

"That I will tell you by-and-bye," answered the young monk, bitterly.

"Prisoner," said the president after having listened to a long and able defence from the counsel appointed for the accused prisoner; "have you anything to add to this defence?"

"My defence, no; for I declare here before heaven that death is preferable to life; but as honour is of more import than life itself, I must endeavour to save mine. Seven years since, Pierre Arbues was raised to the dignity of Grand Inquisitor, he was young and handsome, and of insinuating manners, and men were inclined to believe that he would be less cruel than his predecessors; but, alas! they were deceived, and the most sanguinary dramas continued to be performed before the tribunals of the Inquisition. At that time a noble Catholic family lived in Seville, immensely rich, consisting of three brothers—two of whom had taken holy orders, the third, as brave as the Cid and more beautiful still, was called Fernando—their father, an aged man, a young sister, as pure as an angel, and finally an orphan girl, a distant relation, who loved Fernando and was beloved by him. At their mother's death the Inquisition accused her of heresy, disinterred her body, and confiscated her estates; the father died of grief, during these unjust proceedings; and the children were thrown into prison, one person only was spared, the orphan girl."

"What became of them?" said the judge.

"Do you ask what became of them in the hands of Pierre Arbues? The two eldest and the sister were committed to the flames; but the youngest still lived, and he was preserved for a royal auto-da-fé. Paula, the orphan, who loved Fernando, made an effort to save him; one day she resolved—oh! fatal resolution!—to seek the Grand Inquisitor. It was a dark and dreary day when she entered the gates of the Inquisitorial Palace; she requested an interview with Pierre Arbues, and after being led through various apartments she found herself in the presence of the Inquisitor; the attendant left the room, and closed the door. 'Approach, young maiden,' said the Inquisitor, smitten with her beauty; and she fearlessly drew near to him and threw back her veil, she ▮▮on her knees before him and asked for mercy for her innocent lover; when he heard his name Pierre Arbues' features grew sullen and repulsive; but Paula was beautiful, gentlemen; and the Inquisitor contemplated her kneeling form. 'Rise,' he said, 'the laws of the Inquisition are

severe though just; but I am moved with compassion for you.'   'Heaven bless you,' cried Paula; 'you will save Fernando.'   'Did I say that
young maiden?'   'Oh, do not retract the words you uttered, have pity
on me!'   'And, if I save your lover, what will you do for me?'   Oh,
my lord, my whole life will be at your service; but what can I do for
you who are all powerful?'   'You are beautiful,' said Pierre Arbues,
with a look that terrified Paula; but she dared not let her fear be seen.
The Inquisitor caused her to seat herself beside him on the ottoman on
which he rested. 'Your love for Fernando de Cazalla must be great, would
I could inspire you with one equal to it.   Do you not know,' continued
the Inquisitor, 'that Fernando is intended for the approaching auto-da-
fé, and that he is to be subjected to the torture?'   An exclamation of
intense grief escaped from the breast of Paula—the torture, it was more
dreadful than the scaffold !   'What is the matter?' said the Grand Inquisitor.   'Did you not say Fernando would be subjected to the torture?'
'Yes; but I can save him from it.' Paula breathed more freely.   'Oh,
my lord,' she exclaimed, 'that I might die to serve you!'   'Not die,'
said the Inquisitor, taking Paula's feeble hands in his own, 'not die,
but live; do you not know that Fernando is already condemned to the
stake?'   'Alas! but you can save him,' said the poor girl.   'No; you
alone can save him,' said Pierre Arbues.   'How, my lord; may I die
instead of him?'   'Foolish girl, what need have I of your death; you
you are too beautiful to die;' and with brutal hand he tore the covering
from Paula's bosom.   'Oh! mercy, my lord,' exclaimed the young girl;
'I have no mother, my lord, I am a poor orphan, and have none to look
up to but Fernando;' and she shed a flood of tears, which only increased the violence of the Inquisitor's passion, and springing upon
Paula like a savage lion, he took her up in his sturdy arms and placed
her on the ottoman in a fainting state.   'Be mine,' he cried, 'and I will
save Fernando.'   Pauline rose slowly, and moved towards the door,
'Oh! be accursed!' she cried; 'you can murder Fernando, and I will
die with him.'   'Fernando will die before the auto-da-fé, he is too delicate to endure the torture.'   Poor Paula uttered a despairing cry, and
overcome by the violence of her grief she was completely exhausted.
Pierre Arbues drew her, unresisting, to his seat; 'Nothing can save
Fernando but my will, he said; and I swear by Heaven that I will
save him only on one condition.'   Paula looked wildly round, her reason
tottered—'Do you wish for his life or death?'   She heard not, her eyes
were closed, her heart ceased to beat—'Let Fernando be saved,' she
murmured, in a dying voice."——

Jose was silent; his voice had gradually become weaker, and a cold
perspiration covered his marble forehead.   The judges were filled with
terror, and anxiously awaited the conclusion of this horrible drama.

"A month after this occurrence," continued Jose, "the auto-da-fé
took place.   Anxiously did Paula watch the mournful procession of victims as they moved towards the place of execution, doubtful whether she
should hope or fear after the promise of Pierre Arbues; but the twelfth
victim passed, and she breathed more freely.   Suddenly, a few paces
behind the last of the sufferers, appeared a pale and livid spectre, whose
imbs had been broken and dislocated by the tortures he had undergone;

two priests and two familiars led him forwards, and supported his steps. At first sight, so altered was he, Paula did not recognise him ; but, stretching out his mangled arms towards her, ‘ Paula, Paula !’ he exclaimed, and fell motionless into the arms of the familiar. A cry of piercing anguish escaped from the lips of Paula, and she tried to break through the living barrier of sbirri, but in vain ; then she madly ran through the street, crying out that ‘ she must see the Grand Inquisitor.’ She reached the Grand Place ; there long spires of flame, mingled with clouds of smoke, rose towards the sky—all was over, and the Grand Inquisitor was quietly seated on his throne. ‘ Pierre Arbues,’ exclaimed Paula, ‘ be accursed, and fear my vengeance !’ But no one heeded her, they thought her mad.”

José was silent, and his face, hitherto so pale, turned fiery red, while large drops of perspiration covered his forehead like pearls.

“ Well,” cried the president, moved by curiosity, “ what became of Paula ?”

“ She was avenged ; she it was slew Pierre Arbues.”

“ Explain yourself ; what is there in common between Paula and the young Dominican, José ?”

“ My lord,” continued José, “ I told you Paula swore she would be avenged ; six months afterwards a young man presented himself at the Dominican Convent at Seville, he wished to become a priest. During his noviciate he was noticed by Pierre Arbues, and, out of some capricious feeling, the latter was never happy unless that novice was at his side ; that novice was José !”

“ It was José, then, and not Paula, who killed the Inquisitor.”

“ It was José, and it was Paula ; for Paula and José were the same.”

“ Sacrilege !” exclaimed the judges, when they understood the words of José, “ a double sacrilege ! the holy name of a priest profaned, and a priest assassinated.”

The priests retired, and on their return declared their sentence, to the effect that “ the said Paula should be broken alive on the wheel, afterwards quartered, and that, as a parricide, her right hand should be previously cut off and burned by the executioner ; that, after the execution of the sentence, her limbs should be exposed on the high roads, a prey to the beasts of the field, and no one should be allowed to bury them.”

The unfortunate Paula, when led back to her prison, perceived in the crowd her old nurse Juana. Anxious about the fate of her foster-child, she had left Estevan and Dolores, and returned to Seville.

It was six o’clock in the morning when a man entered the capella, in which Paula had been confined on the night before her execution : it was the executioner.

“ I am ready,” said the young woman, rising from her seat.

The executioner approached her, and having placed on her head a small green cap ornamented with a white cross, he clothed her in a dress one-half red and one-half white.

During her melancholy pilgrimage to the place of execution, Paula was the object of lively curiosity ; all the people pitied her ; they still took her to be a young monk, and they well remembered the odious character of Pierre Arbues. At length the procession reached the Plaza

Mayor. She looked, without shuddering, at the horrible instruments of her punishment, and having piously kissed the silver crucifix offered to her by the priest, the execution began.

The executioner unbound the hands of the victim, and, taking hold of her right hand, placed it on the block, to which he wished to secure it.

" It is unnecessary," she said.

He raised the axe, and rapid as thought it fell; and the fair and delicate hand rolled on the ground, while streams of blood escaped from the wound. Paula grew paler and fainter every instant, and, in spite of her courage, she could scarcely endure her torture.

" Go on," she said ; and the executioner, taking her up in his robust arms, placed her, with the aid of his assistants, upon a large wooden St. Andrew's cross, which lay on the scaffold.

He tied the legs and arms of the victim to the four arms of the cross, and raising a bar of iron in his hands, let it fall heavily on her delicate arm, which broke as if it had been a piece of glass. A low involuntary groan escaped from the lips of the victim, and her whole frame shuddered—it was horrible—and her limbs, in spite of the cords with which they were bound, were agitated with frightful convulsions. Three more blows of the dreadful instrument broke every limb of her beautiful form, and every instant her sighs became less loud and distinct. Soon it was all over—the blood ceased to flow—and Paula's sufferings were at an end.

" She is dead, father," said the executioner to the attendant monk.

" Then Heaven have mercy upon her soul! Pray, brothers, for the soul of the departed."

Juana, who had placed herself at the foot of the scaffold, uttered a deep sigh when she heard these words, as if her breast was relieved of a heavy load ; her child, whom she had been unable to save, had ceased to suffer.

The populace who witnessed this painful scene, when they looked on the meek and patient sufferer, were filled with compassion—how much greater would their admiration have been, had they known it was a woman who endured all this ; but the secret was not known, or it might have given reason to suspect the true cause of Pierre Arbues' death.

The crowd soon dispersed, all but Juana, who remained concealed in a neighbouring church—her task was not yet accomplished.

At length it was night, and the Plaza Mayor was deserted by all, with the exception of several alpargatas, whose task it was to keep watch over the body, and to carry it off after the executioner had performed his task. Juana had purchased the services of these men with all the gold and jewels that remained in her possession.

At ten at night the executioner and his assistants arrived on the spot, the latter bringing with them several sharp-pointed iron rods. Having unbound the corpse, the executioner ripped up with his sharp knife the tunic in which Paula was dressed, and exposed to view her pale and enchanting form ; then, by the light of the red and flickering flame of a torch, he separated the limbs and head with incredible dexterity. As he finished the operation, an elder brother of the Order of Peace and

Charity approached the scaffold, and claimed the victim—it was the privilege of the society. His brethren took the precious booty, and placed it in an oaken coffin—they looked with regret on the abandoned limbs, but justice must have its course—and the executioner, placing the limbs and head in a bag, and followed by his assistants, proceeded towards the Cadiz road, on the other side of the Barrio de Triana. The gardunos followed at a distance. When about half a league distant from Seville, the executioners fixed in the earth five iron spikes, and impaled upon them the limbs and head of the unfortunate Paula, and, having accomplished their task, they retired. The gardunos were concealed at a short distance.

"It is now our turn," said one among them; "but let us make haste, lest the guard should detect us in a robbery like this; I had rather steal the mitre of an archbishop."

They approached the remains of Paula, and, holding out a large white cloth, carefully deposited them in it. A few minutes only were necessary for this operation, and they soon reached the palace of the Garduna; there they were met by Mandamiento.

"Our task is completed, master."

Not yet; follow me;" and he led them to the vault where the body of the governor had been burned.

There Juana awaited them. She took the mangled limbs of Paula from them, and said to Mandamiento—

"Leave me alone for a few minutes; I will bury the remains of my child."

She laid the cloth that contained them upon the ground, and at the sight of the sad relics her courage almost failed her; but, recovering herself, she wiped away her tears, placed the precious remains in the coffin prepared for them, and, covering it with a large veil, knelt before-it.

At the end of an hour Mandamiento returned: Juana rose, and went up to him; then taking a valuable diamond ring from off her finger, she gave it to Mandamiento.

"Signora," he exclaimed, dazzled at the valuable present, "what can I do to acknowledge your incomparable generosity?"

"Leave me until to-morrow with the bier, and then you will bury it in the intended grave."

"Let it be as your ladyship requires," said the master, and Paula's nurse remained alone.

The next day the gardunos entered the vault. They found Juana by the remains of her child; her hands were joined, and her head inclined. They spoke to her; but she answered not—her spirit had fled after that of her child. The gardunos placed her in the coffin along with Paula, and they were buried together in the vaults of the Garduna.

CHAPTER XXIV.

THE ADIEU.

AT one of the numerous inns on the Mole at Cadiz, three persons were in company; around them were numerous necessaries for a voyage beyond the seas; two small trunks and a woollen bag were among them, tied round with cords in such a manner that they could be easily carried by hand, and saved even in case of flight. These three parties were the Count de Vargas, his youthful countess, and John d'Avila; they had been most anxiously awaiting the arrival of José, and the Dutch vessel in which they were about to take their departure was ready to sail by the next tide : nor were they without fear with regard to the Inquisition.

While in this state of anxiety, a loud knock was heard at the door of the room in which they were assembled. Estevan started, and hesitated for a moment.

"Open the door, Senor Don Estevan," cried the new comer.

It was Coco; but José was not with him. He was accompanied by his sister, Manofina, and the serena, and led by one of the brotherhood of Cadiz.

"What has brought you to Cadiz, my children?" said the apostle.

"We have come in search of Senor Don Estevan and the Senora Dolores, to follow in their service," replied the serena.

"You will follow two poor exiles, then, who have scarcely the means of living?"

"Oh, we can work," replied the two women.

"Their seigneuries will have no need of our poor assistance," observed Coco; "José," and the voice of the alguazil grew faint and broken, "José has taken precautions against that." He described the miserable fate of the young monk, and with a trembling hand placed a pocket-book in the hands of Dolores, which she gave to Estevan. It contained a small packet, addressed to Dolores, with directions that it should not be opened until she found herself in safety, and notes to an immense amount, the whole of poor Paula's fortune.

At this instant a sailor came to inform them that the vessel was ready to sail; they took an affectionate farewell of the apostle, and Estevan, Dolores, and the four new comers at once went on board. The vessel bounded gaily through the water, and Cadiz was soon lost to their view. Night came on, and the pale full moon showed its silvery face in the heavens, and lighted up the beautiful features of Dolores, as she reclined her head on the bosom of Estevan. A solemn and religious silence reigned over the vast solitude of the ocean, and the ship rushed through the water with the rapidity of an arrow, and carried the exiles to that distant land where the aurora of liberty is now shining.

FINIS.